About the Author

Clare Reddaway is a Bath-based writer of short stories and plays. Her stories have been widely published online and in anthologies, and she has won and been listed for many short story competitions, including the BBC National Short Story Awards and the Bridport Prize. Clare's plays have been performed throughout the UK, including runs at the Edinburgh Festival and in London and Bath. She has worked for the BBC, Granada Television and various independent production companies, and has volunteered widely. *Dancing in the Shallows* is Clare's debut novel.

Dancing in the Shallows

CLARE REDDAWAY

Fairlight Books

First published by Fairlight Books 2024

Fairlight Books
Summertown Pavilion, 18–24 Middle Way, Oxford, OX2 7LG

A CIP catalogue record for this book is available from the
British Library

1 2 3 4 5 6 7 8 9 10

ISBN 978-1-914148-46-0

www.fairlightbooks.com

Printed and bound in Great Britain by Clays Ltd.

Designed by Sara Wood

Illustrated by Sam Kalda

This is a work of fiction. Names, characters, businesses, events
and incidents are the products of the author's imagination. Any
resemblance to actual persons, living or dead, or actual events
is purely coincidental.

For Auriol

THE PEOPLE WE ARE
GOING TO MEET

Flora Sutherland

Hugh's mother, married to Duncan. Algologist. Lover of and eminent expert in seaweed. Died in the mid-1960s.

Duncan Sutherland

Hugh's father, married to Flora. Advocate and landowner. Died in the late 1950s.

Pat Wintergreen

Cathy's mum. Died two years ago.

Jim Wintergreen

Cathy's dad. Widower. Living it up in Bournemouth.

Hugh Sutherland

Recently deceased. Bram's father, Isla's grandfather. A military man, a lawyer in Inverness. Purchaser of the Skye cottage.

Mairi Sutherland

Hugh's ex-wife, Bram's mother. Passing her retirement in Edinburgh.

Cathy Wintergreen

Isla's mum. Manager of a health care centre in Chippenham.

Bram Sutherland

Isla's father. Lives alone in London.

Isla Wintergreen

Nearly thirty. Searching.

ISLA

POOLS

Chippenham, 2021

Isla lowered herself into the shallow end of the pool. The water was blood-warm, like soup or a half-drunk latte. The smell of chlorine was acrid and chemical. She could feel it scorching the inside of her nose and the tender backs of her knees. The pool was crowded, of course – this was the six o'clock post-work commuter slot. The slow lane was very slow; an elderly man was being overtaken by a sedate trio of middle-aged ladies, their heads held high like carefully coiffed blonde swans. Isla snapped on her goggles and ducked under the rope into the middle lane. The swimmers were faster here, slicing through the water with a certain style. She glanced over at the churning fast lane: capped heads ducking in and out of the water, mouths open, gasping like landed fish. Not for her, not today. There was a space in the steady stream of swimmers in the middle lane. She pushed off.

The email had dropped into her inbox that morning. *They've made an offer*, James said. James Digby, that is, of Brodie, Digby and McDonald, Estate Agents: 'her' estate agents, dealing with 'her' estate. *It's a good offer*, James said, *it's over the asking price. No chain. They'll take the property off your hands and the money will be in your account in no time. Just ping me a confirmation that you want to accept.*

She did want to accept. Of course she did.

She was thrilled that someone wanted to buy it.

She was.

'What's that grandfather of yours doing, leaving you some ruin in the middle of nowhere?' Mum had said. 'It's typical, that's what it is. Bloody typical. Course, if it was down here it would be worth an arm and a leg, but up there... well.'

*

Isla was in a swim queue. The bald man in front of her was doing a proficient overarm crawl, but he was held up by a scrawny bloke with a hipster beard and red trunks doing a jerky breaststroke. Crawl Man couldn't overtake, as he'd crash into the line of swimmers coming the other way, obediently following the designated anticlockwise route. Isla had to be careful that her fingers didn't brush the soles of Crawl Man's feet as he scissored his legs up and down. She also had to be careful he didn't kick her in the face. She slowed her pace. Why couldn't the slow swimmer go into the slow lane? Why couldn't he get out of her way? An unexpected red wave of fury flowed up her body, from her toes to her face. She put it down to the traffic jam, to swim rage. That was surely the explanation.

*

The solicitors had sent her a picture when she'd asked for it, after they'd got in touch. There was an inheritance, they said. From the grandfather she barely knew. He'd left her something in his will. Grandad, Mum's dad, was alive and well and grumbling through his retirement in Bournemouth, tutting about the neighbours and keeping his bungalow spick and span. This other one, this dead grandfather, was linked to her long-gone father, who had deserted her, left her stranded, high and dry, alone with her mother.

The photograph was of a long, low, whitewashed cottage. It had overgrown conifers pressing up against it and scrubby turf in what might have once been a front garden. One of the windows was boarded up and even Isla could see that the line of the slate roof was wonky. The paint was peeling from the front door and the gate was hanging off its hinges. But wild moorland rose straight up behind the cottage, and down to the left Isla could see a dark blue patch of sea.

'It'll be a nice nest egg, I suppose,' said her mum. 'Go towards you putting down a deposit on a flat. Perhaps one of those new ones round the corner. That'd be handy for work, wouldn't it?'

There was no denying it would be handy. Isla could walk to the bus stop and then it was fifteen minutes to the retail park where she worked. She knew each bend and traffic light on that route, because it was the bus she'd taken to school every morning, once she was old enough to go on her own.

'It's not permanent. I'm not going to work at the depot forever, you know,' she said.

'So you say. But you might as well apply for that manager role. Good job security, great benefits. You even get a pension,' Mum said.

'I'm not even thirty! I don't care about my pension.' And yet another Sunday lunch ended with Isla slamming out of the house.

*

'Oi!' It was Crawl Man. Isla hadn't been paying attention and had crashed into him. 'Watch yerself.'

'Sorry, sorry!' said Isla.

'Yer daft pillock...' muttered Crawl Man as he pulled away.

Isla put her head under the water to stop herself screaming.

*

When had she decided to play it all so safe? Why did she depend on her mum's advice? Her mum's sensible, sensible advice. But her mum had been wild once. She'd fallen for Isla's dad after all, out on that Greek island. Isla had seen the photos: her mum in a bikini, lying on the sand, arms round a lanky lad with long black curls, a big smile, his eyes like chips of sky. Isla's eyes. Mum laughing as she jumped out of a boat into a turquoise sea; Mum crawling out of a tent, half-asleep. She'd never let her hair look that messy now. They'd made a go of it for a while when they'd come back home. They even lived in a squat in south London, while Dad worked in clubs in Soho and Mum temped in the West End. Isla couldn't picture her mum in a squat, however hard she tried.

'I was an idiot,' Mum said. 'Falling for him. Feckless, he was. He didn't want to grow up.'

Do as I say, not as I do.

Maybe Isla didn't want to grow up either.

*

Isla plunged her head into the water and swam – three strokes, four, five – the bubbles rising from her lips, dancing to the surface; she held her face underwater until her lungs were empty, until she saw flashes of light behind her eyelids, until she couldn't bear it anymore and she burst up and out, gagging and gasping for breath, flailing her arms and pulling that fresh oxygenated air deep into her lungs. The lifeguard sat up, turned to her, alert. Her breathing slowed, normalised. She started to swim again. The lifeguard slumped back, scratched his thigh, bored.

We regret to inform you that your grandfather died after a short illness at Raigmore Hospital, Inverness.

She'd only met him once, taken north by Dad for an all-too-brief family interlude before Dad vanished again. She was seven. Her memories of her grandfather are of a red face with white bristles, a scratchy green jacket and an elusive smell she later recognised as whisky. What was she supposed to feel now? An old man had died in a hospital far away. Was she supposed to care?

Her grandfather must have known where she was, known her address all this time. The legal letter had arrived swiftly and surely – no false starts, no return to sender, address unknown. It had dropped onto the doormat with no trouble at all. Did he know she had a doormat? That she had a whole life full of jobs and family and friends and doormats that she had built with no help from him or her father at all? If he'd known, why hadn't he ever contacted her? Why hadn't he rescued her? What was this cottage all about? She had the address – she'd looked it up on Google Maps. It was 591 miles away, on the Isle of Skye. There wasn't even a road, let alone the cul-de-sacs, mini-roundabouts and three-lane highways of the town where she lived. There was just a lot of green. And then the blue of the sea.

Why had he left it to her?

What did he expect her to do with it?

*

The hipster hauled himself out of the pool. Crawl Man pulled away. Isla finally had the space to settle into her strokes, pulling herself through the water, stretching out her limbs. The water enveloped her, buoyed her up, cleared her head. This was her element; this brought her joy, calmed and steadied her. She no longer saw the bright turquoise of the municipal pool, blinding in the neon light. She was splashing in the deep, soft, clear water of a mountain pool. She looked down and her kicking legs were sepia from the peat the stream had passed through. She swam to the waterfall and she put her head right into it and she gasped at the power and strength of the torrent as it cascaded off her face and she thrilled at the diamond glitter of the sunshine. She put her toes down and felt the slipperiness of a river rock. She perched precariously – 'Look at me!' she called to Dad. Then she lost her balance and fell back under, but not before she heard a man on the bank laughing. 'She's a natural,' he was saying in that accent that felt strange and familiar at the same time.

*

Was her grandfather sending her a message? Did he know what her life was like? Did he know she'd dropped out of college – she can't remember why now – that she'd taken the first job she could get? And that she'd been drifting ever since, in and out of jobs, in and out of relationships. Some had lasted: she'd been with Gareth for a couple of years – they'd even moved in together, for a while. Her life was good, it was fun, she had friends, she had a good time. But did this grandfather of hers know that when she got into the water, she had a strange yearning, a feeling that she could be somewhere else, someone else? Did he know that?

*

She finished her length and stood up in the shallow end. She saw that Crawl Man was standing too. She watched as he coughed and hawked up a long stream of spit into the pool.

*

She knew then what she was going to do. She was going to go home, and she was going to text her boss at the depot and tell her she had a family emergency. A dead grandfather definitely counted as a family emergency. Then she was going to email James Digby of Brodie, Digby and McDonald and say, no, she didn't accept the offer and she'd like to delay any viewings for the time being, please. Then she was going to pack a bag and she was going to get into her battered little car and drive north, to Skye. She was going to visit her ruin.

Because maybe, just maybe, what her grandfather had given her was a way to escape.

CATHY

AMNIOTIC FLUID

Chippenham, 2019 and London, 1991

'There you are!' Nic stood in the doorway.

Cathy wondered if Nic knew she'd been avoiding her. It's hard to dodge someone in the open-plan reception area of a health centre, but Cathy had done her best. Her mistake had been to go into the tiny break room and switch on the kettle. Now she was trapped.

'Have a look at this!' Nic waved her mobile in her face.

Cathy did not want to have a look. She knew what Nic wanted to show her. Nic had been showing every patient she'd spoken to all morning. It was very unprofessional, Cathy thought. Nic was lucky none of the doctors had seen her. The patients might be coming in for anything – it could be very upsetting. Nic should know better.

'Mia got a DVD and everything,' Nic said. 'Uploaded it onto the computer and sent it over to me last night. On WhatsApp.'

Cathy sighed. There was no escape.

'Go on, then,' she said.

Nic held out her mobile and pressed play. A sepia image appeared on the screen. A scrunched-up face, closed eyes, a hand moving slowly.

'It's 4D. They got it done at Window on the Womb. Had to pay, but Dan said for Mia and the baby, anything is worth it. They're both so excited. Isn't he precious?'

The head turned. Minute fingers curled up and rubbed an eye. The mouth opened in a wide yawn. *What's he got to be tired about*, thought Cathy, *lying around in there?*

A foetus filmed inside a womb. It was scarcely believable.

'Is it definitely a boy, then?' Cathy asked. She had to ask something, although if this was what Nic was like now, goodness knows how she'd behave when the baby was actually born. They'd have to buy a new noticeboard for reception.

'They're going to wait to find out. But I think it's a boy. Look at the size of that head!'

Old wives' tales, and here she is working in a medical centre, thought Cathy. *The sex of the baby has nothing to do with head size.*

'Not like in our day, is it? We'd be lucky to get a black-and-white Instamatic. Still, I was that proud, I pinned mine on the fridge with a magnet. How about you?'

There it was.

'No. I didn't do that,' said Cathy.

*

The gel had been cold on her tummy. She'd felt exposed. Humiliated. She didn't want to be there. She shouldn't be there. She was too young. It wasn't happening; it couldn't be happening.

'Is your husband...' The sonographer glanced at Cathy's notes and pursed her lips. 'Is the father coming?' she asked.

'No,' Cathy said. 'He can't. He's... at work.' The lie stuck in her throat. She started to get up, to swing her legs off the bed, but the sonographer put a hand on her shoulder, pushing her back, firmly.

'It's important to do this,' she said. 'To check baby's growing well.'

So Cathy lay down, tears rising behind her eyelids. She felt like she was at school again, being told off by the teacher. The sonographer placed the probe on her tummy and turned the monitor towards her. A picture appeared on the screen. It was hazy grey-white with a peanut-shaped black area in the centre. Her womb, Cathy assumed. In the black peanut was a head, a body, twig legs bent at tiny knees, arms...

'It's waving,' said Cathy. 'My baby's waving at me.'

'He's having a swim,' said the sonographer. 'He's going to be a champ.'

'Or she?' said Cathy.

'Or she,' agreed the sonographer.

Cathy couldn't take her eyes off the picture. Watching her baby move, its arms and legs fully formed, seeing it stretch and explore, even in grainy black and white, was mesmerising. All this was going on inside her, under the skin, under all that flesh, blood and muscles, cushioned in that balloon of life-giving fluid. It was amazing. Joyous. Cathy was flooded with happiness.

'D'you want a printout?' asked the sonographer. 'To show family?'

Cathy came back down to earth with a crash. Who would she show? Bram was pretending it wasn't happening. He still didn't understand why she hadn't had an abortion. She suspected it would take more than a grainy black-and-white photo to make him come round. And she hadn't told Mum. She couldn't tell her. Mum would be horrified. Mum didn't even know she had a boyfriend and Cathy couldn't see her liking him. Bram didn't have a job or the prospect of a job; he didn't have skills or a plan; he was coasting while he decided what he wanted to do with his life. Mum was a fan of Norman Tebbit and 'get on your bike' – she didn't believe in scroungers. She certainly didn't believe in anarchists. Mum didn't know where Cathy was living. Mum was proper. Tidy and careful and neat. This kind of a mistake would never have happened to her. Mum had warned her. Time and again.

'It's all looking good,' said the sonographer. 'Nothing to worry about here. Your baby is as strong as can be.'

She's going to have to be, thought Cathy. *She's going to have to be a fighter.*

*

Cathy stumbled out of the hospital in a daze. She needed to clear her head, to process what she had just seen. It was the first time she'd realised that she really was growing a baby inside her. She decided to walk home to Vauxhall, even though it was a bit of a way and she'd usually go by Tube. The sun was out so she took a shortcut across Archbishop's Park. She wasn't usually in a park on a weekday – she was usually at work, busy in one of the offices Brook Street Bureau sent her to. Bram thought it was bourgeois and sexist to be a secretary, but Cathy enjoyed it and she was good at it. She liked being able to type up a perfectly laid-out letter without once using Tipp-Ex; she liked being able to answer the phone with crisp efficiency and put the caller through to the right number without cutting them off; she even liked the orderliness of filing. She thought it was lucky she'd learnt secretarial skills at school. The Bureau were pleased with her, telling her that she was one of their best temps. They promised that the next time a permanent job came up, she'd be the first in line, if that's what she wanted. So far she'd liked the excitement of not knowing where she'd be from week to week. But now she worried about maternity leave and maternity pay, and how she'd carry on if she had a baby – who would watch it during the day; how she would pay them; and how she would look after a baby, when she had no idea whatsoever what to do with it, since she'd never even held one and didn't know one end of a nappy from the other. Cathy was suddenly so tired that she couldn't take another step. She sat down on a bench and closed her eyes.

She jerked awake when she felt someone tugging at her handbag. Instinctively, she grabbed it tighter and shrieked when she realised that two young lads on bikes were right on top of her, trying to steal it. One had hold of her bag, and the other one was shoving at her. She tried to get up, to push back at them, but she was trapped by the bikes. One of the boys karate-chopped her hand and she had to let go of the handle. The other lad tugged hard and the bag came free. He hooked it on his handlebars and they both launched away, pedalling hard. Cathy set off in pursuit, screaming at them, but her ankle boots had high heels and her skirt was tight, and she tripped and fell to her knees, grazing her skin. Blood bubbled through her torn tights. The boys disappeared into the distance.

There were plenty of people around – mums with pushchairs, an elderly couple sitting on a neighbouring bench. No one helped her. No one even looked at her.

*

She was sitting on the front steps of the house when Bram eventually came home.

'You're late,' she said, and she burst into tears. 'They took the picture,' she howled. 'Of our baby.'

To be fair to Bram, and sometimes she did want to be fair to him, he was gentleness itself that evening. He carried her inside and up to the rooms that they shared with a bunch of other people – some friends of Bram's, some friends of friends, some strangers who'd heard about the place on the grapevine. He laid her down on their mattress and he made her a cup of tea. He remembered that she liked two sugars. He even managed to get some fresh milk. Cathy thought he must have nicked it from next door's doorstep, as they never had fresh milk. He sat down beside her and stroked her hair.

'Why didn't you come to the hospital with me?' she asked.

'I had to go and see a bloke about a job,' he said.

'Have you got it?'

'Looks like it,' he said. 'But don't you worry about that now.' He started to sing what sounded like a Gaelic lullaby as he painted her face with his fingers.

She thought of how much she loved him as she drifted off to sleep.

*

Cathy's waters broke when she was standing at the sink. She was turning and turning the tap, and nothing was coming out, and then she felt a wet stream down her leg and at first she thought, *How peculiar*, there must be a leak in the pipe and the water must be coming out at her somehow from the cupboard under the sink, and then she realised that there wasn't a cupboard under the sink, just a jumble of old pipes and piles of filthy rags, and that the water to the squat had been cut off again and that she was about to go into labour.

She was on her own in the house. It was seven o'clock in the evening. She supposed the others were at the pub. She didn't know where Bram had got to. He'd been late a lot recently. He said it was something to do with the bands he was working with. 'Musicians' hours', he called it. She didn't question him. She couldn't face being called bourgeois again.

She had done a bit of planning. She'd gone as far as to get a book out of the library. It was supposed to be a '*Complete Guide for All Parents-To-Be*', but mainly she'd read about whether her baby was growing eyelashes or fingernails this week and stroked her bump. She'd glanced at the section that said she should have a bag packed and ready for when she went into labour, but she wasn't due for another three weeks and she'd thought she had plenty of time. Perhaps she hadn't believed it would ever really happen. Now, as she stumbled into their bedroom, she wasn't thinking very clearly; there was a gnawing pain in her belly, like the cramps that she got with her period. She saw a Sainsbury's carrier bag and stuffed a nightdress into it. She found the sponge bag she'd taken to Greece and she put in a toothbrush and some toothpaste. She added a flannel. She couldn't think what else she'd need. She got to the front door before she realised that her trousers were still soaking wet. She turned back to change and as she pulled on a pair of pregnancy leggings, a jagged pain made her double over and gasp. She'd better hurry up. As she headed out, she bumped into the pallets they used as their kitchen table. It reminded her that she should leave a note for Bram.

Gone to hospital, come quick, she wrote on a piece of paper which she left on top of the pallets.

As she closed the door behind her, the draught made the paper float off the table and land face down on the floor.

*

When she got to the main road, two taxis drove straight past her. She doubled over three times before one stopped.

'St Thomas's Hospital,' she said to the driver. 'I'm going to have a baby.'

'Not in my cab you're not, love,' he said, and he put his foot on the accelerator, racing through red lights to get her to the maternity unit.

'Your fella meeting you there?' he asked as he leant back to open the door.

'No,' she said. When she reached for her purse, he waved her away.

'Just call it Raymond if it's a boy,' he said, and she grinned, even though the pains were getting stronger now.

*

Later, she could only remember snapshots.

A crowded ward.

Women moaning. Writhing.

Men huddled over them.

Screams in the distance.

A monitor by her bed, a wire taped to her belly.

The baby's heartbeat. Bright green peaks on a dark blue background.

Beep. Beep. Beep.

Alive.

The midwife, cheery, large, a mole on her cheek. Holding her hand. Whispering in her ear.

'You can do it. You can do it. You can do it.'

Whispering.

'Have you got a birth partner? Is there someone we can call?'

Giving her the telephone number of the Old Red Lion, the pub on the corner – they would sometimes pass a message on to the house where she lived, which didn't have a telephone as it didn't have proper electricity, only the electricity that Aemon had rerouted from next door.

The minute hand on the clock. The hour hand. Clicking. Round and round and round.

Panting.

Pain.

Panting.

Pain.

Neon strip lights.

Maroon hexagonal patterns on the curtains.

Cracks in the ceiling.

Texture of the sheet under her fingers. Rough. Nubbly.

How much longer?

Pain.

How much longer?

Pain.

How could she bear it?

Pain.

She couldn't bear it.

Wheeled into the labour unit.

Lights.

Faces.

'Is there anyone else? How about your mum?'

And she gave them her number, the phone number of the house where she'd lived for most of her life – until the last year, when she hadn't been there at all – the number that came easily to her, the number that tripped off her tongue, her home.

'Is she coming?'

'She's coming,' said the midwife. 'Now, push.'

And Cathy pushed and screamed, and pushed and screamed, and then there she was, her baby, her beautiful baby, wiped and wrapped and laid on her chest, and Cathy stared and stared at her.

'What's her name?' said the midwife.

It floated into her head and Cathy decided there and then.

'Isla,' she said.

*

When Cathy woke up, Mum was sitting by the bedside. She was wearing her coat, that blue tweed one that Cathy knew so well, and her driving shoes. Her handbag was on her lap and she was holding it with one hand. The other hand was holding Cathy's.

'Hello, Mum,' said Cathy.

'Hello, pet,' said her mum. 'Haven't you been busy? You've got ever such a beautiful baby.' Cathy looked over to the other side of the bed and there was the cot with Isla wrapped in a warm white blanket. She was asleep.

'Oh, Mum. I'm sorry I didn't tell you.'

'Well. I'm here now.'

'I thought… I thought you'd be angry…'

Her mum leant over and gave her a kiss.

'I was ever so worried about you. We hadn't seen you for so long.'

'I'm sorry.'

'So where is he? The father?' Cathy saw her mum squeeze her lips so tightly that they turned white, and she realised that she was right to think her mum would be angry. It was just that Mum wasn't angry with her.

'You'll meet him. When we go home,' said Cathy, and her eyelids drifted closed because she'd been in labour for hours and hours, and she was so, so tired, and it was all too much to deal with right now, particularly when all she wanted to think about was how perfect her baby was. Hers.

Cathy had to stay in hospital for an extra night and Mum didn't leave her side, except to visit Mothercare. She clucked when Cathy said she'd not got anything for the baby, nothing at all, and she'd said she'd go and get some essentials. They'd go together once Cathy was up to it, but there were things that the baby needed straight away. Mum came back with nappies and bottles and muslins and the sweetest clothes Cathy had ever seen. Tiny Babygros covered in moons and stars, a little knitted bonnet, something fluffy Mum said was a sleepsuit, and two warm blankets. She also bought a bright-pink car seat and this was what they strapped Isla into the next day, when Cathy was allowed to leave.

Cathy couldn't believe she was the same person who'd come to the ward what felt like months ago. She found it difficult to walk – her legs were like wet noodles. When she stepped out of the hospital, she didn't recognise the world. Why had she never noticed there was so much danger? People were shoving and knocking and pushing against her; they could swoop in on their bicycles and grab the handle of the car seat – it would be so easy to steal her baby away. Buses and cars were giant balls of fiery metal hurtling towards them and one slight moment of distraction – and who hadn't been distracted when driving – would mean the baby crushed beneath their wheels. Even the dank London air seemed laced with ice. Isla was so tiny and so vulnerable and so easy to break, and Cathy realised there was no way she could keep her alive. She bent down over the car seat so her Mum wouldn't see her tears as she tucked an extra blanket around her infinitely fragile, vulnerable baby.

'This way,' said Mum. She picked up the car seat and linked her arm with Cathy's, leading her to the familiar red Peugeot.

'Dad let you have the car?' she said.

'Just this once,' said Mum, and she clipped the baby seat into the front as if she'd been doing it all her life. Then she got behind the wheel.

'Where are we going?' Mum said. She paused. 'We never got your address. Just those postcards. We thought you might live in Big Ben, you sent us that many pictures of it!' She laughed, but Cathy knew that she was hurt, and the surge of guilt nearly overwhelmed her.

*

It was when Mum drew up outside the house in Vauxhall and neatly manoeuvred the Peugeot into a space beside a parking meter that Cathy started to panic. She hadn't thought this through.

'This looks nice,' said Mum, as she took in the line of red-brick Victorian houses.

'It's the one on the end,' said Cathy.

'Oh,' said Mum, and Cathy saw the house with new eyes. The rotten tooth in the terrace. The sapling growing out of the cracked front steps; the filthy windows, their broken panes covered over with cardboard. She led Mum in and up the stairs. The walls were mouldy and Aaron had added some new graffiti. The banister was hanging from its fastenings. There were piles of rubbish.

'These stairs won't be fun with a buggy,' said her mum. 'You should get your landlord to tidy all of this up. It's a fire hazard.'

'We're not exactly renting,' said Cathy and she pushed open the door to their rooms.

There were puddles of water everywhere.

Bram had his back to the door. He was barefoot. His trousers were rolled up and his T-shirt filthy. He was mopping. He glanced over his shoulder.

'You left the bloody taps on. Look at it!'

'Bram, this is—' But her mum didn't let her finish.

'How dare you? How *dare* you speak to my daughter like that, young man?' Bram sprang round. 'After all she's been through!' Bram took in Cathy's mum, and he also took in the car seat.

'Mum! Let me—'

'I didn't know where you'd gone.'

'Couldn't be bothered to get to the hospital! If I hadn't been there, she'd have been all alone!'

'I thought you'd left—'

'Disgraceful! Neglecting her like that!'

'Mum! Stop it! Bram, what about the note—'

'Didn't you think? Didn't you even think to check?'

Cathy looked at Bram, at this person she'd been living with for months and months. And instead of the ethereal charmer who had wooed her on a Greek beach – such a contrast to the lager lads she knew at home – instead of him she saw a scrawny, pale boy whose Adam's apple was jerking up and down in his throat as he tried not to cry. And Cathy, too, questioned why he hadn't wondered where she'd gone, hadn't bothered to check the hospital.

'Is that...?' he said as he looked at the car seat.

'I had the baby,' said Cathy, uselessly.

He took a step towards them.

'Oh no you don't!' said Mum. 'Not like that. You're filthy!'

'How was it? Are you all right? Is the baby OK?' asked Bram.

'Is this where you're going to keep her?' said Mum. 'And with this...' Mum looked Bram up and down, and it was absolutely plain that she found him wanting.

'A little girl?' he said.

'This is no place for a baby. Seriously, Catherine, look at it,' and Mum swept her arm wide. 'It'll be the death of her!'

Cathy looked round. The room did indeed look squalid. The sofa that they'd found by a skip and dragged up the stairs with triumph now looked torn and shabby, and the water had left a tidemark on the stained green arms. The bare boards were splintered and studded with nails, and the kitchenette was dingy and depressing, the sink coming away from the wall.

Was this really a safe place to bring up a baby?

Mum must have sensed Cathy wavering.

'How about coming home for a few days? Get you settled into a routine. I'll be there to give you a helping hand. It's warm and clean at home. We need to make sure baby's eating properly. They can lose weight in a flash, you know, and then you're in trouble.'

'Maybe for a few days...' said Cathy.

'Stay until you know what you're doing. You need a bit of pampering after what you've been through.'

Mum was edging Cathy towards the door. Slowly. Inexorably.

'Don't go...' Bram said.

'He can visit,' conceded Mum. 'Once you've settled down.'

Cathy was torn. There was Bram, who only last week had been the centre of her world – but now

40

there was this other person, this tiny squally blob of a thing who needed her, depended on her and her alone, and whom Cathy loved in a way she'd never loved anything ever before.

'Please stay! We can do this together,' pleaded Bram.

Cathy moved towards the door.

'I can get food. I can scrub this place top to bottom if that's what you want—'

'You haven't got a clue,' said Mum and she glared at him. 'Do you know how to get a baby to sleep? What would you do about colic? Do you even know what meningitis looks like?'

'I can find out, I can learn—'

'I'll take baby,' Mum said to Cathy. 'You go on down to the car.'

Now that Cathy had made her choice, she was clattering down the stairs.

'Does she have a name?' called Bram from the top of the stairs.

'Isla,' Cathy called back, and she was out of the front door and into the Peugeot before she could change her mind.

*

The kettle in the break room was boiling. Cathy took the *KEEP CALM AND CARRY ON* mug from the cupboard. It was not her favourite. She put in a teabag and poured in the boiling water. She didn't take two sugars anymore. She was watching her figure. She took a bottle of milk out of the fridge and sniffed it. She approved of the surgery having a milkman and glass bottles, but it did mean the milk went off quickly. This one seemed all right, so she added a splash.

She looked back at Nic's mobile.

'You should print out one of those scan pictures. Pin it up on the noticeboard. That'll cheer us all up.' She smiled at Nic, but the smile came nowhere near her eyes. 'Everyone loves a baby. Don't they.'

A PHONE CALL

London and Chippenham, 1998

'So where is she?'
*I've been looking forward
to this. So much.*

'I told you. She has ballet
now on Wednesdays.'
*You've haven't
rung for weeks.*

'Every Wednesday?'

'Well, yes, during
term time. She doesn't
have it in the holidays
or at half-term—'

'And when's half-term?'
*You should tell me.
I'm her dad.*

'Half-term is when
it always is.'

*You've got that smug
parent superiority.*

'How am I supposed
to know? It's different
in Scotland!'

Keeping things from me.

You could look it up.

Like I'm not important.

*You'd know if you
rang more.*

Like I don't matter.

'I was looking forward
to talking to her.'

'Of course.'

'Maybe I could come to
watch her do ballet?'

'Maybe you could.'
You never will.

I could, I could...

'I bet she's brilliant. Bet
she's elegant and... jumpy...
and goes up on those points
like Darcey Bussell—'

'She's a little young for that.
Is there anything else?'

'I haven't spoken to
her for weeks.'

Whose fault is that?

'I wanted to hear her voice.'

We're here.

I want to know her.

'I'm not stopping you.'

'But you are! Don't you
see? You've sent her to
ballet! Without telling me!'

Why would I tell you?

*She has a whole
life without me.*

How would I tell you?

*She has hobbies and
classes and friends
and bloody activities
with pointy shoes.*

'She likes ballet. It
makes her happy. I didn't
think you'd mind.'

'I do!'
*I want to take her fishing.
Take her climbing in
the mountains.
Take her to the opera.
Take her to Rome.*

45

Show her the world.
Show her my world.
'Is she any good at it?'

'Does it matter?'

'Tell her I rang.'
Of course you won't.

'You will tell her, won't
you? Hey, why doesn't she
ring *me*, when she gets in?'

'She'll be too tired. She'll
have her tea and then bed.'

Her timetable's more
complicated than the
Prime Minister's.

The schedule, the routine…
I need it.

You'll make her a
suburban conformist.
Like mother, like daughter.

You have no idea
how hard it is.

How hard can it be?

The orderly, careful structure.

Built to keep me out.

Built to keep me sane.

'She's going to think
I don't care.'

Do you care?

I do care. I do.
I miss her. I miss her.
I miss you.
'She's going to forget
me. Isn't she?'

'She has nothing to forget.'

Cathy puts the receiver down gently, the click of
buttons severing the line.
She leans her forehead against the wall.
She closes her eyes.

Bram lets the black handset dangle on its silver cord.
He leans his forehead against the cold glass of the
phone box.
He breathes in the stink of piss.
In. Out. In. Out.

BRAM

RIPPLES

Inverness, 2020

It was not the funeral Bram had imagined.

The minister, Sandy McRae, had not shaken his hand, had not touched him at all. Over his cassock, McRae was wearing improvised plastic PPE and a Perspex face shield: he looked like he was about to deactivate a nuclear reactor rather than lead a service. Bram could see his eyes. They were wide with fear. The funeral director had not allowed Bram to carry his father's coffin. It would not be possible to maintain the two-metre safe distance, he'd said.

Bram was the only mourner. He stood in the front pew of the kirk with his mask clamped thickly over his nose and mouth, his gloved hands fumbling with the order of service. There would be no hymns. It wasn't safe to sing.

He had insisted on a proper church service, then a committal of the coffin into a neatly dug grave. His father hadn't made his choices known and Bram thought that he'd want the respectability of the churchyard. *HERE LIES HUGH SUTHERLAND*. But now he wondered whether he was right. Whether a quick cremation and a memorial sometime in the future would have been better. Then his friends could have come to pay their respects. After all, Dad did have friends. Mum would have turned out, divorce or no divorce, but not now, not when she was so vulnerable. Bram should have listened to the funeral director during the agonising Zoom meeting the week before.

'Which coffin would you like, sir? For a gentleman of Mr Sutherland's standing,' he'd said, holding up samples for Bram to peer at, 'we do recommend the oak.'

*

Bram had driven up to Inverness a couple of days before the funeral. The roads were empty. It was eerie, as if World War Three had broken out and no one had told him. He had the email from McRae on his phone, in case he was stopped by the police, in case he needed to justify why he was travelling. Date and time of the service, *FUNERAL* in capital letters. Even with no traffic, the drive had taken hours and hours, but there was nowhere to break the journey – nothing was open. He'd felt light-headed with exhaustion when he arrived at the house. He unlocked the door with the key that was always kept under the doormat and almost called out, until he remembered that Dad wasn't there. That he was dead.

The house was the same as it had always been. Faded rugs, 1970s crockery, an ancient TV, everything covered with a thin layer of dust. Bram could see the indentation on the sofa where Dad had sat for so many years, as if he had just stood up and walked out of the room. Both Dad and Bram had kept up the pretence that Dad wouldn't be away long, so he only took essentials. A neighbour had come in with a list. His dad had wanted a black metal box from under his bed, the neighbour told Bram. That and some spare pyjamas. He didn't need much.

Dad had been in the home since February. The decision had come quickly in the end. Bram had been suggesting a move for years, perhaps to sheltered housing, to a more convenient flat. The stairs had long been too much for Dad and he had retreated to the ground floor. Then he'd had a fall, broken his hip. He'd lain by the front door until the postman found him. A care home was the only answer, Bram had insisted. It wasn't like he could look after his father himself, not all the way from London. It wasn't forever. Just until the hip healed and he got his mobility back. Bram had been pleased and surprised when Dad had agreed.

It took the pressure off. No need to worry now; he'd be safe in the home.

*

Bram chose Chopin for the entry of the coffin into the church. It was a piece that Dad had played on the piano when Bram was a child. It reminded him of rainy Sunday afternoons, the smell of furniture polish and roast chicken. The organist was shielding, so Bram had brought a CD from Dad's house. McRae had found an old portable player which still worked, after a fashion. The sound didn't fill the church. Even Bram could barely hear it. Discreet, unobtrusive, decorous. Like Dad.

*

By the time Bram visited the home, the country was in lockdown. He wasn't allowed to go in. He stood in the garden and talked to Dad through the window. Dad looked frail, sitting in an armchair, but he was dressed and smiling, and he looked clean and neat. His hair was brushed and he'd shaved, or someone had shaved him.

Bram peered past into his room. It was impersonal, except for three photographs, propped up on a shelf. Bram on a beach in Greece, smiling at the camera, more tanned than he'd ever been before or since. A picture of Mum, sitting on a rocky beach with Bram as a baby in her lap. And there was one of Dad from his army days, somewhere in the Middle East if the desert was anything to go by. He was standing with a buddy, an arm slung over his shoulder.

Bram thought there was something of the barracks about the room. As if Dad had reverted to his quarters in the desert. Orderly. Shipshape. The years of family, of women and children, the years of divorce had been stripped away and he'd gone back to that time after the war. His arm around a buddy.

'Lovely daffs,' Dad said. 'Nearly over now.'

'It looks like they keep the gardens well. Nice to have a view of hills,' Bram said. 'I'd walk you round if they'd let me.'

'I know,' said Dad. 'Don't get cold out there. There's a chill wind.'

Just the one visit.

So much left unsaid.

*

'When you throw a stone into water, the water is disturbed, and ripples appear. You can't see the stone anymore, but you can see the effect, as the ripples spread across the surface.'

What was the minister talking about? Ripples? What had ripples got to do with his father? The reading had been from Matthew, something about Jesus and His disciples; the minister had chosen it, had decided it was appropriate. Perhaps McRae thought he was a ripple. Bram stifled a snort of laughter. Dad would like that.

*

Covid had whipped round the home like a lick of spit.

The night after they told him, Bram woke up with the sheets drenched in sweat. He was gasping, shuddering, taking great lungfuls of air as deep and oxygen-rich as he possibly could. He saw Dad in that room in the home. Saw him struggling to breathe. Saw his eyes, saw that he was trapped and his breath was ragged, desperate. He saw the muscles in Dad's neck strain like the ropes on a sail and he heard that sound, that rasp, and he saw Dad reach out his hand, heard him call his name...

Bram knew he wouldn't sleep again that night.

He shouldn't have sent Dad to the home. He should have driven up through the night – bugger the lock-down, bugger the police, bugger the bloody buggering rules – and he should have smashed that window and climbed in and lifted Dad out and into his car and carried him away to safety. He should have rescued Dad and set him down on the seashore with the salt wind in his hair. That's what he should have done.

But he didn't.

He'd been relieved. He'd been pleased not to have the responsibility. The whole time-consuming worry and bother of caring.

He let his dad stay there. He let him die. He let him die alone.

*

Bram slumped forward in the pew. Minister McRae probably thought that he was praying.

He was not.

What bowed his head was shame. The memory of his failure, all the times he should have behaved better, with more compassion and more kindness. All the things he should have said. The questions he should have asked. The times he should have broken down barriers, not built them up. How he hoped he would do things differently if he had his time again. How he feared he would not.

This was a funeral thick with regret.

*

'...in sure and certain hope of the Resurrection to eternal life,' said the minister. They were outside. The coffin had been lowered into the ground. Dad's coffin. The funeral director wiped a trowel with sanitiser and placed it so that Bram could reach it, then stood back, out of germs' way. Bram took a scoop of soil from the heap beside the open grave and scattered it down onto the oak coffin lid. The splattering sound was flat and final.

*

Bram stood by the grave for a long time, long after the minister had sidled away and the funeral director had left to go to his next death. He stood there as the dusk rolled in and the lights in the surrounding streets came on. He stayed even as a gentle rain began to fall.

Eternal life was too long and temporal life was too short.

He had failed his father, and now his father was dead. But he was a father himself. He had his daughter.

*

He'd read the will. He'd seen what his father had done. He'd been surprised. At first he thought it was a gift for Isla. Now he wondered if it was a gorgeous, glorious gift for him.

He could break the pattern. He could choose to reach out, to create a relationship – a better, stronger, richer relationship than the one he had had with his own father.

It wasn't too late. Was it?

'I'm sorry, Dad,' he whispered. 'I'm sorry about everything.'

He turned and left the churchyard, the mud from his father's grave caught in the tread of his shoes.

FREE MEN

Skye, 2016

Bram is up a ladder. He has balanced a pot of limewash on the top step and is dipping a wide brush into the paint. He taps it against the side of the tin, reaches up and places the brush under the eaves, then pulls down firmly, leaving a bright white streak on the outside wall of his dad's cottage.

It is satisfying.

He dips the brush in again and paints another streak, then another. Gradually, he covers the whole of the façade, carefully painting around the window frames and the front door. By the time he climbs down the ladder and steps back to look at his handiwork, the cottage is brighter and cleaner, and the muscles in his arms and his back ache as though he's done a vigorous workout at the gym.

Hugh puts down the shears where he has been clipping the hedge and examines the new paintwork.

'Not bad,' he says.

Bram will take that praise from his father.

'Beer?' he says and when Hugh nods, Bram gets a couple of bottles from the fridge, clips off the tops and brings them outside. The midges are not swarming yet, so Hugh can sit on the bench, placed to take full advantage of the setting sun and the view over the sea loch to Macleod's Tables on the other side of the bay. The mountains look imposing, but Bram knows they are more of a scramble than an actual rock climb and that the view from Healabhal Mhòr is spectacular. Maybe he should have a day of hiking while he's here. For the first time since he arrived, Bram feels positive. It must be because he's been out in the open air, accomplishing something tangible.

'I could do this,' he says. 'Painting and decorating. I like it. It's physical, it's rewarding, you don't need to take your work home at the end of the day. I should move into the cottage, take it up full time.'

Hugh looks at him. Bram gets that familiar sour feeling that he's a disappointment.

'You wouldn't be able to behave here the way you do down in London,' Hugh says.

'What way is that, Dad?'

'With all your women,' says Hugh.

Bram starts to breathe faster. He arrived in Skye a couple of nights ago to join his father for a week's break. He was supposed to bring his partner, but she didn't come with him. Hugh hasn't asked him why. He simply shifted the activities from sightseeing to house maintenance.

'It's not lots of women. It's one woman. Her name is Mya, as well you know.'

'Yes. Mya. Of course,' says Hugh.

'Although, for your information, it's not her anymore. She left me.' Bram takes a gulp of beer but he swallows too much and it goes down the wrong way. He chooses to believe that the tears in his eyes are purely from choking.

'Ah.'

'Is that it? Ah? I thought you liked her!'

'Oh, I did. Charming woman.'

Bram thinks back to Mya, a whirl of fury as she blew through his flat, throwing her belongings into a holdall as she ranted about selfishness and emotional unavailability and being let down, yet again. He counted himself lucky to have got away with a couple of broken plates and no actual injuries. Charming is not the word he'd have chosen.

'She's decided to go back to New York,' he says.

'Sorry to hear that,' says Hugh. 'Still, I suppose the lure of the bright lights, Broadway and all that.'

'That's not why she left.'

'No? Still, can't be helped, eh. Here's to not being tied down.' Hugh leans over and chinks his bottle of beer with Bram's. 'To being free men!'

Hugh leans over and tops up Bram's whisky. They are in Hugh's study in Inverness. Bram is in his twenties. He has driven up from London and he is distraught. He has poured out the story of how his girlfriend has fled their life together; how her mother turned up out of the blue, condemning the place they lived in as too dirty, too dangerous; how they'd taken the baby away. 'What should I do?' says Bram. 'Should I follow her? I didn't hold the baby – I didn't even see her. All I know is she's called Isla—'

'Do you know where they've gone?'

'To Cathy's parents' house—'

'Where is that?'

'Somewhere in the south-west... I think it's not far from Bristol.'

'We could look in the telephone directory, search for the family. It's not impossible.'

Bram swishes the amber liquid round and round in his glass. The light catches the cut crystal.

'I don't know her full name,' he says.

'I see.'

'No! No, you don't! We were – we didn't want all that bourgeois life that you... We just wanted to be Bram and Cathy, living in our own bubble. It's only a squat but it's ours.'

Hugh shifts in his chair, but Bram keeps talking: 'We are – we were – in love...'

'It sounds to me as though you've had a lucky escape.' Hugh chinks his glass with Bram's. 'Here's to being free men!'

The chink of glasses.

Free men together.

*

'That's what you said before, Dad, do you remember?' Bram takes another swig of his beer and looks out over the sunset sea.

'When was that?'

'When I came to see you. After Isla was born. You told me not to follow her, to let her be.'

Hugh rubs the back of his ear.

'I did not tell you not to follow her. That's where you landed up. All by yourself.'

'That's not how I remember it.'

'Of course not. We never do.' Hugh smooths his trousers. 'You were so young.'

'Not too young.'

'Debatable.'

Bram thinks back. He *was* young. He was new to London and he'd finally got the freedom he'd longed for through all those years of school and study. He'd wanted to go out and meet strangers and create music and stay up until the wee small hours and sleep on a floor miles from his own, if that's where he washed up. He didn't want the baby. He didn't want to think about breast milk and colic and nappies and the dark fear of keeping something alive.

'You said I'd have another chance. That I had plenty of time for family. Years and years and years. But, I don't know… I feel like those years have slipped through my fingers.'

'I can't read the future,' says Hugh. 'I wish I could.' He runs his finger round the top of the beer bottle. 'The thing is, we don't always get what we want. We don't always make the right decisions. We have to live with that. All of us.'

Bram looks at his dad and wonders whether he's still talking about Isla.

*

Bram is ten. He is sitting at the table in the cottage in Skye, kicking his feet against the legs of his chair. It's the holidays and he's having a supper of fish fingers, mash and peas with his mum and dad.

'Can we go fishing tonight, Dad?' he asks.

'No,' says his younger dad, with his more luxuriant hair and his smooth face, free from liver spots.

'But it's still light. We haven't been out in the boat today – can we, can we, can we, pleeeease?'

'Why don't you take the boy?' says his mother at the other end of the table. Unlike his father, she is looking haggard, her hair unbrushed and her eyes red-rimmed.

'The tide is too low.'

'You could launch here and I could pick you both up down at the village.'

'I need to top up the engine oil.'

'There's a can in the shed.'

His father cuts a segment of fish finger and puts it in his mouth. He chews it and swallows. The sound of masticating is deafening in the silence.

Bram looks from one parent to the other.

This has nothing to do with the boat.

The air is pinging with bitterness and recriminations.

'I don't need to go fishing,' says Bram. 'I can stay here. I can finish that jigsaw...'

Dad places his knife and fork together on the plate. He pushes back his chair, making a scraping noise that sets Bram's teeth on edge.

'I'm going for a walk.' Dad shrugs on a waxed jacket. He steps out of the door, closing it carefully behind him.

Tears seep out of his mother's eyes.

'Sorry, Mum,' says Bram.

'Eat your peas,' she says, and she lights a cigarette, dropping the ash into her unfinished supper.

That was the worst summer. By Christmas his parents had separated, and he was bouncing back and forth between their homes and his boarding-school dorm. By the next year, he'd started his annual holiday in Skye with Dad for a week in July or August. His mother didn't come along, although she was invited. It was all very civilised. Bram was glad that the tension had gone, but he did see that Dad was sad sometimes. He'd memorise the best jokes from school and tell them to Dad to cheer him up. It didn't always work.

*

'The thing is, Dad, I don't think I want to be a free man. I don't think I'm very good at it. I was happy with Mya. We had a great life together.'

'She obviously didn't think so,' says Hugh.

'Thanks!' says Bram, but he knows that Hugh is right. He'd held back, like he always did. Afraid that he would be abandoned. Afraid his heart would be broken. It's easier never to take that step than take the step and get punched in the gut when you get it wrong.

'I wish I'd done things differently.'

'Has she definitely finished with you?'

Bram thinks of those final words, spat in his face. 'You have steel around your heart. You are a shell of a man!'

'Oh, yes. Definitely.'

'You'll want to change the locks. Can't have her coming back and helping herself.'

'She's not like that—'

'You can't be too careful. Do you need the name of a good locksmith?'

'I can find a locksmith!'

The sunset has painted the sea deep red and pink and orange. A perfect romantic backdrop. Mya would have loved it.

'It's not about Mya, really. The end of her and me – that's sad, of course. But it's more… It's that I look back now, and I worry I threw away the one thing that mattered, the one thing that might have lasted.'

'The baby?'

'Well, she's a young woman now.'

'So get in touch! Find Isla and ring her up. Write her a letter! It can't be that difficult.'

Bram looks down at his paint-splattered fingers.

'I did. She sent the letter back.'

'You didn't say.'

'Wasn't much point. It was years ago. Cathy said Isla didn't want to hear from me.'

'When she was a teenager? You don't want to set much store by that. Remember when you were that age?'

'I wasn't that bad. You overreacted.' Bram recalls his dad's disgust at his leather jacket and earrings.

He wonders how Isla expressed her teen angst. He supposes he'll never know. 'It's too late. I've nothing to offer her.'

'People can change.'

'Did you ever change?' Bram asks. As far back as Bram can remember, Dad has always been Dad: military-stiff, straight-laced.

'I did my best.'

Hugh lifts up his binoculars and follows a whimbrel as it flies north. It dips behind a headland, out of sight, but Hugh keeps the lenses fixed on the far distance. Bram wonders what he's watching. At last, he puts down the binoculars.

'Do you love this place?' says Hugh.

Bram sighs. What did he expect? His father doesn't do personal.

'You said earlier you might move here, set up as a painter-decorator.'

'It's a middle-of-the-night pipe dream, Dad,' Bram says. 'I'm embedded down south. The job pays well and I know what I'm doing. I've got friends.' It sounds empty and sad when he says it out loud.

'I see.'

'Why?'

'Nothing. I was just thinking.'

'Right.' Bram stands up. 'Well. Thanks for the sympathy and the advice, as ever.'

He strides towards the cottage. He's had years of this. Dad doesn't listen. He doesn't care. And when the advice does come, it's wrong. He could have had the chance – why didn't he chase her? Why didn't he run down the stairs, and grab her and grab the baby and drag them back into his life? Why didn't he – why didn't he? – and now it's too late, *too late*. Bram's hands clench into fists and, with a grunting roar, he throws his bottle hard at the fresh white paint. The bottle smashes, leaving a wet brown beer stain on the clean wall.

The moment of violence leaves him winded.

Hugh turns his head, his eyes mild.

'Get me another if you go to the fridge,' he says.

Bram crunches over the glass into the cool darkness of the cottage.

*

When Bram comes back out, he hands Dad a bottle and sits down.

'Looks like it's going to be a fine day tomorrow,' says Hugh. 'We could take the boat out.'

'OK, Dad,' says Bram. 'Let's do that.'

He picks up the binoculars and stares out over the sea.

ISLA AND BRAM

THE COLD LIGHT OF DAY

Skye, 2021

'You have arrived at your destination.'

I don't think so, thought Isla. *This is nowhere. What's the satnav talking about?*

She pulled over to the side of the single-lane road. Scrubby grass. Three enormous sheep. They had all stopped eating and they were staring at her. Surely sheep weren't normally that big. Were sheep dangerous? Did they attack?

She stared the lead sheep squarely in the eyes. It became shifty. It tossed its head and lowered its mouth to the ground.

You can't kid me with all that grass-munching, thought Isla. *You were sassing me. But I won. Ha!*

She looked around. *There's nothing here*, she thought. She must be in the wrong place. She sighed. She felt like her head was full of cotton wool. She'd set off yesterday from Wiltshire and driven up the spine of England, overnighting at the cheapest motorway service station she could find, then on up through the Lowlands and the Highlands of Scotland to the Isle of Skye. As she drove, the landscape had become wilder and emptier. Mountains rose sheer from the side of the roads, valleys were pocked with lakes, and houses were few and far between. Traffic became sparser: end-to-end cars had been replaced by camper vans and sturdy trucks. The pace had slowed. When she'd crossed the bridge that linked the mainland to Skye, she'd had to stop the car to stare. On one side was a field with shaggy orange cattle sporting comically curly horns, and on the other, mountains with jagged ridges tumbled into a sea splattered with islands. The sea wasn't blue like in Greece or Spain, but it did sparkle where the sun caught the tips of the waves. Isla had never seen anything so enticing.

She'd driven on, across the island, high up over a pass with spiked peaks on the left and moorland on the right. The road met the west coast and meandered north, until it got to here. Wherever here was.

She looked again at the instructions that the estate agent, James Digby, had sent.

Turn left after a 'Logs for Sale' sign. The gate will be open. It's half a mile down the lane. Hope your suspension is good.

What lane? thought Isla. She peered. There was an old gate, and perhaps that was a sort of track. *What the hell*, she thought, and she swung left, and bumped and jumped the car down the hill until she got to a small group of conifers with a wooden gate propped open. She drove through.

And there it was.

The cottage. Her cottage. Her inheritance.

It looked a bit of a mess. A big mess, in fact.

Isla shivered.

Maybe it was that clouds had blown across the sun and there was a faint drizzle. She'd expected the odd window to be boarded up, the paint to be peeling and the roof to be sagging, but she'd also expected – well, for the place to sing to her. And it wasn't doing that.

It looked cold and damp and unfriendly. As did the man standing by the front door. She got out of the car.

'Isla Wintergreen?'

The man was middle-aged, with thin sandy hair. He made no effort to conceal his impatience.

'Are you James Digby?'

'I was expecting you an hour and a half ago.'

'I did ring,' Isla said. 'Left a message.'

'Oh, there's no reception here,' he said.

'I'm sorry,' Isla said and she was sorry, but equally, she'd been driving for hours and hours, was bone tired, and she wanted to have a pee and a stretch. A glass of water and a biscuit wouldn't have gone amiss, or even a cup of tea...

'You'd better come in. I'm afraid it's in a bit of a state.' He took out some keys and unlocked the front door.

'This is the main room, kitchen through there, all in need of major renovation – nothing's been done for years.'

'It's lovely,' said Isla. It really wasn't. It was dark and dank and there was a funny smell, like that time Scraps had chased a mouse under the floorboards and it had died and no one could get at it, and eventually Mum had had to get a carpenter to take the floorboards up and wrap the body in newspaper and take it away. It was that kind of a smell.

'The stairs are through the back. You'll want to go up.'

Obediently, Isla climbed the stairs. She had to duck to avoid the beams.

It was dark and damp up here too. She opened a door and flicked on a light. She was surprised that it worked. A bedroom. Looked like a man's room, something about the dingy colours – brown wood headboard, dark cupboards. This must have been where her grandfather slept. She flicked the switch off again.

The bathroom was across the other side of the stairs. Isla poked her head in. Basic, utilitarian. A toilet. Her bladder clenched. There was nothing for it. She headed in, crouched, peed. The release was glorious. Footsteps came up the stairs. James Digby's face appeared, vanishing the moment he saw her.

'Marking your territory, then,' he muttered as he stomped back down.

Well, that was fucking rude, Isla thought, and she kicked the door closed. A new bolt and a couple of screws. She could do that. An easy fix.

She pulled the ancient chain, taking a step back in case the cistern crashed down on her head. Water flushed into the bowl.

*

James Digby was standing on the doorstep when she came back into the main room. His face was tight with disapproval.

'Your buyers have found another property,' he said. 'It's a shame to have lost them. A property of this type can be hard to sell.'

'I wanted to see it for myself,' said Isla. She refused to apologise to him again. She suspected he knew she'd never dealt with an estate agent before. Perhaps he didn't have many clients her age. Twenty-nine. Nearly thirty. So nearly thirty.

'Well. Can't be helped, I suppose. What are your plans going forward?' Why did everyone always bloody well ask her that? It was almost like they knew.

'I'm just visiting,' said Isla.

'For how long?'

'The weekend. A few days. A week at most.'

'We would like some clarity. We're coming up to the best time of year to sell – we'll be very busy. The tourists arrive, fall in love with Skye, decide to buy an old wreck, happens every year—'

'Old wreck?'

He gave a little cough. 'A property in need of development. One person's old wreck is another person's idyll.'

An idyll. An escape. Was that what she needed?

'So, I would recommend that you don't leave it too long. The roof might not survive another winter's storms.'

'What about the contents?' she asked.

'Oh, we'll get the house-clearance people in once the sale's gone through. The buyers are unlikely to want all this—' He stopped himself this time, before he said 'rubbish'. 'Most of it can go in a skip. Once you've taken your mementoes, of course. You'll want something to remember your grandfather by.'

'Of course,' she said. Isla didn't tell him that she'd only met her grandfather once, when she was seven, that this bequest had come out of the blue. It was a bit like winning the lottery. If the lottery doled out tumbledown Scottish cottages and was run by your estranged father's family.

'Well, if you're staying then I'd better be on my way. Things to do, clients to see.' He handed her a bunch of keys. 'They're all here. Why don't you just drop 'em off at the office when you leave?'

He got into his red Land Rover, did a neat three-point turn, drove out through the gate and bounced up over the lane towards the road.

Isla was alone.

'We would like some clarity,' she mimicked to herself. 'Stuck-up, patronising... grrr...'

She turned back and surveyed the main room. It ran the length of the front of the cottage. Her room at Mum's house – where she was currently back living, yet again – could slide into this space twice over, easily. She paced it out. Her room and her mum's room. Not bad.

This room was dominated by a picture of a stag over the fireplace. He was standing on a mountainside, with crags and a lake in the background, and storm clouds brewing over the peaks. The stag's antlers were huge. He was the colour of a burnished conker and he looked proud and grand, and frankly a little bit arrogant. Gathered round the fireplace were a battered leather sofa and a couple of ancient armchairs. A worn rug lay on the stone-flagged floor. At the other end of the room was a table, with five mismatched chairs. There was a cupboard in the corner, a couple of faded prints on the walls and a bookcase full of books.

Isla decided to give the stag a closer look. As she walked over, she bumped into a ceramic vase perching on a side table. The vase tottered – she grabbed it just before it fell. So close. She set the vase carefully back on the table and looked at it. It was a particularly unpleasant mix of liver and green swirls.

Then Isla realised. *It's my vase*, she thought. *I can do whatever I want with it.*

She picked it up and dropped it, very deliberately, onto the floor, where it broke into two very satisfying halves. She started to laugh. Maybe this could be fun.

She thought of her belongings, packed into boxes when she moved out of the flat she'd rented with Gareth – the flat she couldn't afford on one salary. She didn't own a sofa, didn't have a table. She pulled back the curtains at the windows. Hey – she owned curtains! Her very own curtains! She started to open drawers and cupboards, began to take things out. What else could she now say was hers?

*

What started as an exploration of what she now owned became an exploration of who had once owned it. It was as if someone had walked out of the door one day and never come back. There were clothes in wardrobes: a green tweed jacket with patched elbows, a pair of brogues with wooden shoe trees preserving their shape. There were books: paperback thrillers by Robert Harris and John le Carré; detective stories by Agatha Christie and Ngaio Marsh; factual books about geology and the Clearances; a well-thumbed paperback about the legends of Skye. There was a pair of binoculars beside a birdwatching book. All of which pointed to one person, the kind of person that Isla had encountered in her years as a waitress: a man with a braying voice and an entitled manner. And then there were other things that muddied the picture. A bumper box of condoms, half-empty. Who had her grandfather been fucking? A couple of volumes of poetry, by Rabbie Burns and Jackie Kay. A set of black silk sheets, in their original packaging. Unopened, but still. This grandfather of hers had had a life here and it was a life that was a bit confusing.

'You'd know,' Isla said to the stag. During her rummaging, she'd found a large bottle of whisky at the back of a kitchen cupboard. She poured herself a generous measure. She flung the tweed jacket over her shoulders, liking the scratchy feeling of it on her neck and its faint lingering smell of woodsmoke.

'What have you seen? What was he like?'

There was an old record player sitting at the bottom of one of the bookcases. It might still work. She pulled it out and plugged it in. She picked a record at random from a pile – *The Best of Django Reinhardt* – and put it on the turntable, setting the needle onto the outside groove.

'Who was he dancing with?' she said as the strains of jazz filled the air.

The stag said nothing.

She laughed and she danced and she chatted to the stag until she made herself dizzy and had to drag herself upstairs to the bedroom. She toppled forward onto the covers and fell asleep.

*

In Edinburgh, Bram was sitting with his mother, playing chess and sipping a glass of sherry. He moved his knight and immediately regretted it. Mairi was winning, as she always did, and he was wondering whether he could suggest that they play something else – anything else – when he got a text.

'Sorry, I should look at this,' he said, hoping that it would give him time to plot a strategy. He clicked on the text.

Isla Wintergreen is at Taobh na Mara for an unspecified period. She arrived today. You wanted me to let you know. James Digby.

Bram looked at the text. Adrenalin surged through his body. He didn't recognise the emotion at first. Then it dawned on him. It was hope.

'There's been a change of plan,' he said. 'I have to go up to Skye. First thing.'

'That'll be nice, dear,' said Mairi. 'Checkmate.'

*

Isla startled awake and sat bolt upright.

What the fuck was that?

A noise. Downstairs.

There it was again.

A sort of scraping.

Like something being dragged across the floor.

It was nothing.

What was being dragged across the floor?

Nothing serious.

Who was dragging something across the floor?

She could check it in the morning.

Like a man dragging a dead body, its shoes scraping and bumping across the wood floor.

She had to check it now.

She wrapped a blanket around her and crept across the room.

She needed a weapon.

Her hairbrush.

Better than nothing.

Not much better than nothing.

And her phone.

In case she needed the police.

Or a torch.

Or to bludgeon someone to death.

It was 3am.

It was light.

Not very light.

But light.

At 3am.

She crept down the stairs, hairbrush and phone held out in front of her like drawn daggers.

She could hear the blood from her heart pulsing in her ears.

She could hear her breath, shallow, panting.

She could hear each step on each floorboard when she needed to be silent, as silent as the night.

The scrape came again.

It was outside the back door.

She crept to the door.

If she opened the door, whatever was outside could get in.

She put her ear against the door.

Scrape.

Fingernails against wood.

'Hello?' she whispered.

Scrape.

What was outside?

What was it?

She couldn't see.

She couldn't see without opening the door.

There was nothing for it.

She pulled back the bolt and flung open the door, brandishing her hairbrush and her torch.

'Arrrggghhhhhhh!'

There was nothing there.

Just a shrub. A shrub that was overgrown and straggly.

A shrub that was very close to the door.

A shrub that had one long, thin bent branch, the tip of which touched the outside of the door. Earlier today the weather had been still and balmy. A sea wind had got up in the night. As the wind blew the branch, it rasped against the door.

It made a sound like fingernails.

Like a body being dragged across the floor.

It was a branch.

It was only a branch.

Isla sank down on the doorstep, wrapped the blanket around herself. She was shaking. She wanted to go home. She wanted her mum.

What on earth was she doing here?

*

The next morning Isla woke late. Her head was pounding. She lay still for a moment. She was in her grandfather's bed, looking up at her grandfather's ceiling, with a hangover from her grandfather's whisky. She wondered what he'd have thought of that. She hoped he would have approved.

She sat up gingerly. The room was full of sunlight. The terrors of the night seemed far away. She staggered to the window. The cottage looked out over a long, thin sea loch. She could see a tiny post van driving along a road on the other side, and above the road, two mountains looming up: one with a flat top and one with a more contoured shape. They both glowed golden in the sunshine. Perhaps they provided some kind of shelter for the sea – there didn't seem to be a lot of waves out there. The cottage was built on a slope covered with brambles and bracken, but she noticed the traces of what looked like a path down to the water. That's what she'd do: she'd go for a swim. That would make her feel better.

As she stepped out of the front door, she stopped. Her dad must have spent his summers here. He must have run out of this door, across the drive, to the path. He must have pushed through the brambles and bracken, and down to the sea, like she was about to do. She could see the chubby legs of a small boy, hear his whoops of joy; they caught in her throat. She wished she'd come here when she was a child. She'd loved the holidays with her mum at the seaside in Dorset or Devon, but this felt wilder, more remote, less safe – definitely less safe. Isla wondered if she'd have been different, if this landscape and this sea were part of her. Who would she be? Could she still be that person?

She pushed her way down to the shore, thwacking the brambles and pushing through the bracken. She found herself on a small shingle beach: it was almost like it was her very own. The tide was out and the water was dark with seaweed. There was a jetty with a slipway, sloping down into the waves. She grinned. This was a bit different from the municipal pool. This water was steely and black, rippled with waves. No lane markers here, no chlorine or strip lighting. And there was so much space.

She stripped down to her costume. She looked around. She was entirely alone. Why not? She slid out of her swimsuit. She ran down the slipway and launched into the sea. The water was like a slap in the face, so cold it made her jaw ache and her skin tingle hot, but the fizz of being naked in the water was like drinking champagne. She held still for a moment to let herself acclimatise, then swam. Her strokes smoothed and lengthened. She felt the water work on her, her hangover fall away and her head soothe. She flipped over onto her back and stared up at the sky, pale blue with wisps of white cloud. *Imagine being able to do this every morning. To walk out of your home and down to the sea. Imagine.*

She turned back to the shore. She shouldn't stay in long; the water was too cold. It'd take her a few weeks to get used to it. She caught herself. *A few weeks?*

As she swam back, she saw that a small blue van had parked on the verge of the tarmacked lane that ran down to the slipway. She hadn't noticed the lane, hadn't heard the van pull up. The driver's door opened, and a man got out and stretched. A weather-beaten face, drawstring cotton trousers, bare feet. He was about her age, not bad-looking. Nice flat stomach, bit of a tan, a blue tattoo snaking around his torso. He looked like he'd just woken up.

She trod water. She couldn't get out without him seeing her. She couldn't stay in because she'd get hypothermia. She could see her towel and her clothes. Maybe he hadn't noticed her.

The man raised a hand and nodded. He'd seen her.

Sod it.

She took a deep breath and swam onto the slipway, standing straight up out of the water in a fluid movement and striding to her clothes, head held high. She rubbed herself down vigorously. She was pulling on her T-shirt when the man in the van said: 'You're quite the swimmer.'

Isla gave a tight smile. 'There's no need to watch.'

'You were in my field of vision,' he said. 'Made my day.'

Isla pulled on her jeans. If her teeth hadn't been chattering, she'd have gritted them.

'You should take care. There's ropes under there, for the boats that moor in the bay.'

'Yes. I saw,' she said.

'I'm Luke, by the way,' he said. 'Fancy a cuppa?'

He'd set a kettle on a camping stove. She realised that she was cold, deep inside, and ravenous. She'd had nothing to eat the night before, only the whisky. She'd have killed for a cup of tea. With a lump of sugar. Maybe two.

'Certainly not,' she said as she pushed her feet into her shoes. She gathered up her towel and costume, and swept past him with as much dignity as she could muster.

'See you around, Flipper,' said Luke as he settled back to look out over the water.

*

It was still dark when Bram left Edinburgh. It was a long drive to Skye but he didn't mind. He had plenty to think about on the journey, a whole future to plan.

He pulled in at a service station to top up his petrol. As he walked into the shop to pay, he realised he was about to greet his daughter empty-handed, with nothing to give her after all these years. He looked at the shelves of near out-of-date chocolates; he turned away from the cheap alcohol. Could he give her a book? The paperbacks on offer had been sitting out for too long, their covers bendy from the damp, and they all seemed to be true crime, a series of increasingly torrid serial killers. Then near the counter he saw a display of flowers. That would be perfect! There were pink carnations, a couple of bunches of mixed tulips, and roses – red ones and yellow ones. Red roses were for romance, he thought. That would send quite the wrong message, and besides, he loved yellow roses. They might well be his favourite flowers, now he thought about it. He selected a bunch and went up to the cashier to pay.

'They're for my daughter,' he said.

'Nice,' said the cashier. 'Cash or card?'

Bram laid the flowers carefully on the passenger seat. He drummed his fingers in time to the Schubert on the radio and smiled as he drove on into the sunrise.

*

Isla pushed open the front door of the cottage and went into the main room. It certainly showed signs of her presence, the table groaning with the contents of the cupboards: records, crockery, a vintage album full of what looked like pressed seaweed lying open on top of piles of clothes. She nodded to the stag and saw that someone had drawn a speech bubble above his mouth, and the words: 'Mine's a half!' Someone. That would be her. She could hazily remember doing it, frustrated by the stag's refusal to talk back. She'd have to clean it off later. Or not. It was hers after all. Maybe the speech bubble gave the stag a bit of raffish street cred.

She pulled on her coat and grabbed her car keys. Food. Essential. Later she'd try to get the hot water to work so she could have a shower, but if she didn't eat something very soon, she'd pass out.

As she pulled into the petrol station (much closer than she'd thought – she could even walk it if she had to, if she really had to), she hit a patch of signal. Her phone pinged. Then pinged and pinged and pinged.

Mum: Are you OK?

Mum: Let me know you've arrived. I don't know what you think you're doing.

Siobhan: Hope you are coping with your family emergency. I've put you in for a shift on Friday morning.

Mum: Are you running away? Like you always do? It won't help, you know.

Siobhan: Please confirm that you've received this message.

Mum: Nothing will be easier up there than it is down here.

Pippa: Hi babe. I've got some news! Fancy a coffee this week? (I'll be on the decaf!!!) xxxx

Mum: Worried I haven't heard. When are you coming back?

Isla put her phone back in her pocket and went into the petrol station. This wasn't like any petrol station she knew – it looked like it would cover all your household needs. Coal, windscreen wash and fresh bread; whisky, cauliflowers and boat hooks, all tumbled in together. Isla took a basket and filled it – cereal, milk, bread, cheese, baked beans, pasta, bacon. That would do for now. As she took it to the counter, she saw a noticeboard covered in cards. *Old school*, she thought as she glanced at them. In among *Guitar and rabbit hutch for sale* and *French lessons offered* there was a card with *Cleaner needed for Airbnb property* and another that said *Housekeeper wanted – good rates*.

Isla slid her basket onto the counter.

'Morning,' she said.

'Morning.' The woman behind the counter looked about Isla's age. Judging by the size of her belly, she must have been at least eight months pregnant. 'You staying at Taobh na Mara?'

'Yes,' said Isla. How did the woman know?

'Lovely down there,' said the woman.

'Yes,' said Isla. Then, on impulse: 'Have you always lived here?'

'Aye. I went to Glasgow for college but I didn't take to it,' she said. 'Too many people. Everyone angry all the time.'

'D'you like it on the island?' Isla couldn't believe she'd asked – it was so nosy.

The woman paused. Looked at her.

'You thinking of staying?' she asked.

'Oh, no. No, no, no. Not at all. I couldn't,' Isla said.

'You should come down to the village tonight. There's a band playing in the hall.' The woman put the shopping in a brown paper bag. 'You'd have to keep your clothes on, though.'

'What?' said Isla. She looked at the woman, who raised her eyebrows.

Isla laughed. 'News travels fast.'

The woman grinned. 'That'll be £12.50.'

'Thanks. I'll think about the band,' said Isla as she paid.

Before she left, she went back to the noticeboard and snapped a photo of the cards.

*

Isla sat in the car and scrolled through the messages. She texted Mum.

Isla: I'm here, all good, no reception at cottage, not running away, what do you mean?? More later.

She was sure she knew what her best friend Pippa's news would be. Pippa had been trying for a baby for ages. Isla sighed. That was just peachy.

Isla: In Scotland babe. Back soon. Can't wait to hear your news! Love ya.

And then there was Siobhan. Her harried, anxious, irritable boss. Isla had a twinge of guilt. Viewing the cottage was hardly a family emergency. But what was she supposed to say? It's not like they ever let her take any time off. It was a shit job. If she lost it, she could always get another shit job. There were plenty of those out there. It was the ones you might enjoy that were thin on the ground.

Isla: Hi Siobhan. Signal terrible. Won't get back this week, loads of family stuff, big trauma, really sorry :(

The phone pinged almost immediately.

Siobhan: You have my sympathy. However, if I don't see you on Friday morning I will need to escalate this.

Mum would be furious.

Isla switched off her phone.

*

Isla went back to the cottage. She managed to fire up the boiler, but the water would take a while to heat up. She pulled on an extra fleece and the tweed jacket from last night. She'd put a couple of slices of bread in the toaster and was frying some bacon when there was a knock on the door. She opened it.

A man was standing outside, holding a bunch of flowers.

'Isla?' he said.

'Yes.'

'Hello,' Bram said. She could see him take a deep breath. 'I'm your father.'

Isla stared. When she'd pestered her, her mother had shown her blurry photographs of her dad: a young man with curly black hair, laughing on a beach – a scrawny boy, really. Her mum had always said he had blue, blue eyes. The man in front of her didn't have wild curls, and his eyes were grey, but there was something familiar about the shape of his face, the turn of his lips.

'What do you want?' she said.

'You've grown,' he said, and he smiled. She flushed. She tried to remember when she'd last seen him. It was years and years and years. And now he'd just turned up, without any warning. She hadn't had a shower. She was wearing two jumpers and two pairs of socks, and his father's tweed coat.

'Can I come in?' he asked. 'These are for you.' He held out the flowers. Plastic-wrapped roses, already drooping. She'd seen the exact same bunch in a bucket at the petrol station. He'd obviously put a lot of thought into it, then.

She took them and stood back. He stepped into the room and looked around. He laughed.

'I see you've made yourself at home,' he said.

Isla's breath came faster. Of course. He hadn't come to see her. He didn't care about her. It was the house.

'Why shouldn't I?' she said.

'The stag's a distinct improvement,' he said. He had a definite air of ownership.

'This is my house now – it's all legal. You can't just show up here!' She could feel her face flaming red.

'I wanted to see you. There's so much I want to say to you—'

'If you'd wanted to see me, why didn't you ever come before? To my home?'

'I tried—'

'Why now? And how did you know I was here?'

'James told me—'

'James Digby? The estate agent? Isn't there some kind of confidentiality thing between—'

'No, not really, I've known him for years.'

'So you could drop everything and come here but never to—' Her words were tumbling out of her, hot and hurt.

'I was in Edinburgh, my mother's not been well, your grandmother—'

'Grandmother? So now I have a grandmother too, do I?'

'Of course you do!'

'Well, how am I to know? How am I to know anything?'

She whacked him in the chest with the flowers, snapping the roses' heads in the process. He took a step back. His foot crunched on something. He looked down. It was the vase that she'd smashed the night before. Isla thought that she might either cry or explode.

'I'm sorry, OK? It fell. I didn't mean to break it! I suppose it's valuable or a family heirloom or something – I didn't know it was there! It's not like—'

'Don't worry, it's nothing.'

'I bumped into it. I'd been driving and driving, I was tired!'

'It was a horrible vase—'

'I didn't mean to! I don't understand – why are you here?'

Bram sighed.

'I wanted… I need to… could we perhaps… sit down for a moment?' Then, 'Is there something burning?'

Isla stared at him, then ran into the kitchen. The bacon was black.

'Fuck,' she said. 'I was starving.'

'Pass me that tin and I'll heat you some beans if you make me a coffee,' said Bram.

Isla picked up the frying pan and tipped the bacon into the bin. She put the pan back on the cooker. She leant against the counter. She took a deep, calming breath.

'Look. I don't know why you've come, but I can imagine. You think that this shouldn't be mine. That you should have inherited the cottage.'

'No, I—'

'That I'm an outsider and I shouldn't be here. Well, you're probably right.'

'You misunderstand—'

'But it is mine, and it's mine by law. So I'd like you to leave,' she said.

Bram looked like he'd been kicked in the chest. Isla realised that this cottage must contain his childhood memories, of holidays and family and fun. She unbent for a moment.

'You could take a couple of things, if you want, to remember your father by, or the place, whatever. I think that's reasonable. Don't you?'

Bram rubbed one finger along the countertop. He swallowed.

'Yes. Very reasonable.'

'So, please feel free to choose,' she said.

She'd spent so many years imagining what she'd say to her father if she met him again. This was definitely not part of the script. But she didn't know how to reel it back in.

Bram wandered out into the main room. She saw him looking at the open book.

'You found the seaweed album. It was made by my grandmother. Your great-grandmother, I suppose. She became quite an eminent biologist, you know. After the First World War.'

Isla had been beginning to soften, but all vestiges of sympathy vanished.

'No. I didn't know. I had no idea that my great-grandmother was an eminent scientist. How would I? Who on earth do you think would have told me?'

'I'm sorry...'

'Go on, take it! If it's so important! If she was such a fantastic eminent scientist!'

'That's not what I meant—'

'What did you mean?'

'You should have it. I just wanted you to know what it was.'

Bram ran his hand through his hair. He looked defeated.

'I'll take one of the pairs of binoculars, if I may. He used them all the time up here. And...' He hesitated. There was something, but he wondered if it would make everything worse.

'Yes?'

'His jacket,' Bram said and he nodded at the tweed which Isla had slung over her two fleeces.

Isla flushed. She took the jacket off, breathing in the smell of woodsmoke and whisky. She passed it to her father.

Bram took the jacket.

'Thank you. I'm sorry. I've handled this so badly.'

Isla looked down.

'I wonder, can I have your phone number? I'd like to call you sometime. Start over. Perhaps I could take you out to supper. We could talk. Maybe you'd like to meet your grandmother.'

Isla stared at him. Her eyes were swimming with tears. Bram took a notebook and pen out of his pocket and handed them to her.

'Please,' he said.

Numbly, she flicked to an empty page. She wrote down her number. She handed the notebook and pen back to him.

'Thank you,' he said. 'Again, I'm sorry. This didn't go the way I had imagined.' He turned and stepped out of the cottage.

Isla heard the car door slam, the engine start. She heard him reverse, then turn and drive up the lane to the road. It was only as the sound was dying away that she followed him out into the drive.

'Wait...' she whispered. It was too late – he'd gone.

*

She went back into the cottage.

This was her house and she had every right to be here.

She was not going to allow this to deter her.

She was not going to allow him to deter her.

She liked it here. She liked walking down to swim in the wild sea; she liked the stag picture, and the creaks and groans of the cottage; she liked going to the petrol station to buy a loaf of bread. Maybe this place could work for her – maybe it was what she was looking for. Maybe not forever, maybe not for long at all, but it was worth a try, at least for a while.

She would ring the numbers she'd got from the noticeboard. See about the cleaning job and the housekeeping job. She would find out if there was a bar or a café in the village that needed an extra pair of hands, particularly now summer was coming.

She would go to the village tonight. She would buy herself a beer and she would laugh in the faces of those locals who'd heard that she'd been skinny-dipping. She'd dance and she'd laugh and she'd forget about her father, and she'd think about her future and her hopes and her dreams. Then she'd walk back to her own cottage in that strange pale half-light of the night.

But first, there was something she had to do. She opened all the drawers in the kitchen until she found some heavy scissors. She unlocked the back door. That branch looked so innocent in the daylight, bending prettily, carefree, brushing teasingly against the door and the wall.

She took the scissors and she hacked through the branch where it joined the main trunk of the shrub. Then she threw it as far away as she possibly could.

She went into the cottage and closed the door behind her.

FLORA

GUTWEED AND BLADDERWRACK

Sandsend, Whitby, 1910

She hurried down to the water's edge. She should be able to reach the rocks easily before Duncan woke up.

Lay aside for a time all thought of conventional appearances, and be content to support the weight of a pair of boy's shooting boots.

She'd borrowed her boots from her younger brother. She'd had to stuff the toes with rags.

'Planning to look glamorous on your honeymoon, I see,' he'd teased.

She splashed through the shallows, skipping over those rippling waves.

Feel the luxury of not having to be afraid of your boots; neither of wetting nor destroying them. Feel all the comfort of walking steadily forward, the very strength of the soles making your tread firm.

Her stride *was* firm, it *was* steady! The boots made her walk differently, more confidently. Or maybe it was because she'd hitched up her skirts in such a wayward manner. *Let the petticoats never come below the ankle.* It was a delight to be able to move so easily, to feel the breeze on her legs.

She'd left her shawl on the picnic rug beside Duncan. It would only get sodden on her expedition. The straw hat she was wearing was secured firmly by a bow tied under her chin.

All millinery work – silks, satins, lace, bracelets and other jewellery – must, and will be, laid aside.

She'd taken off the jet brooch Duncan had given her, pinning it to the shawl. It would be a shame to lose it, even if it was heavy and clumpy and ugly. Now her only jewellery was her bright new wedding ring. She hadn't brought a stick, although Mrs Alfred Gatty, authoress, said it was an essential piece of equipment for the quest. Flora knew that if she carried a stick everyone around her would fuss, especially Duncan.

The basket may be lined with gutta-percha, or exchanged, by those who care to invest in it, for an Indian-rubber bag, which can be strapped round the waist.

Her bag was a simple cloth receptacle. It would have to do.

Flora looked around her with a naturalist's eye. She didn't think much of the wash-up. The high-water mark had left hardly any interesting samples. It had to be because of the abnormally fine weather they had been experiencing. She wondered whether she was the first honeymooner ever to long for strong winds and stormy weather, as they brought so much in from the sea. Still, even with the sunshine, she had high hopes for the cliffs at the far end of the beach. It was why she had suggested today's expedition to Sandsend. She thought there would be rock pools, and she'd even spotted some caves, ripe for exploration.

*

Exploration. To Flora, there was no word more enticing. She had always dreamt of faraway lands. Of feeling sun so hot it was hard to breathe, of galloping towards mirages shimmering over desert sands, of rowing down limpid rivers brushed by overhanging creepers, of crunching through glittering snows as mountain peaks disappeared above her into the clouds. She'd only read about these wonders in books. She'd envied her eldest brother Edwin when he'd joined the merchant navy, and waited impatiently for his letters, breathing in the spices and perfumes she was sure were caught in their folds. But she herself had never been more than a day's train ride from Edinburgh.

*

The first pool that she reached was a crevice in some boulders that had trapped stray waves from the retreating tide.

> *Some ... will be crystal basins, not thickly crowded and confused with plants, exquisitely clean and refined, lined with a lilac-pink* **Melohesian** *incrustation perhaps, or graced at the bottom or sides by a few elegant tufts of, now and then, the exquisite little* **Polysiphonia parasitica,** *or the deep green* **Bryopsis plumosa,** *displaying their feathery forms to the best advantage.*

She peered in and couldn't see anything that was lilac-pink or deep green. There were only a couple of discarded shells and some glossy pebbles.

So far today she'd identified two species of seaweed and they were both ones which she already had in her collection. The first, which even her trusty boots had slipped on, was *Fucus vesiculosus*. It was very far from rare. Her father called it bladderwrack and it lay in great heaps of slimy olive strands on every shoreline she'd ever visited. She liked its air bubbles, which were such fun to jump on and pop. Bladderwrack was the first seaweed she had harvested and pasted into her scrapbook. The other specimen was coating the round boulders in lime-green hair. It was *Ulva intestinalis*. Gutweed.

She thought of Duncan's hand on her belly, the palm rough and heavy against her goose-pimpled skin. She thought of how it made something twist deep in her gut, made her want to squirm away, and how she had to clench her teeth to stop herself from crying out. She thought of how, later, she had lain in the bath with her hair floating around her until the water cooled and Duncan called for her to come to breakfast or she'd catch a chill.

She was lucky. She was so, so lucky. She must remember that.

*

She scrambled on, heading for the base of the cliffs, and nearly tumbled into another pool. This one was perfect. It was a whole wild world laid out in vivid miniature, with forests and caves and rivers and plains. It was deep and varied, with sunny uplands and shaded patches. She saw blood-red anemones, their tendrils waving. Half a bleached crab shell.

Barnacled limpets clinging to the steep sides. A black shape darted across the bottom, disappearing into the darkness of a crevice. Most importantly, there were so many seaweeds. This was one of the *hanging gardens of the sea* which her book had promised.

She knelt down on the edge of the rocks and reached into the water.

The prettiest things are not to be got at without trouble.

She carefully lifted up the fronds of green gutweed and peered underneath. Yes! There was a pinkish-mauve clump with chalky tips that was hiding shyly – a patch of *Corallina officinalis*! She stroked the fronds, holding them flat against her palm in the water. Each strand was a miniature tree, with trunks and branches and branchlets. *More beautiful than any flower*, she thought. She took a knife from her bag and carefully cut some samples. She put them in her bag. She didn't take the whole plant. She wanted to leave it to thrive.

She worked her way round the pool, reaching beneath plants and rocks, exploring the furthest reaches of her new territory. When she was certain that the pool had revealed all its secrets, she sat back on her heels. She looked back at the spot where she'd left Duncan, her husband of three weeks, asleep on the sand. She could go back now. She should go back now. She looked over at the cliffs. She could see the sun bouncing off the surface of more pools, glinting, tempting. What new specimens might they contain?

She turned away from the beach and headed the other way, towards the cliffs.

*

'Flora? Flora! *Flora!*'

She was on her knees, with both hands deep in water, when she heard him calling. She stood up and saw him in the distance, a dumpy ginger-haired figure hurrying across the sands towards her. She waved, and he waved back, an urgent jerky action. He was pointing. She turned to look.

The tide had come in.

He'd reached the edge of the rocks now and was hopping from boulder to boulder in his bare feet, his trousers rolled up to his plump white knees. He teetered and lost his balance, putting one foot right into a pool. She giggled, then put her hand over her mouth. He wouldn't like to be laughed at.

She didn't want to stop her shore-hunting. The rock pools had yielded some seaweeds that she'd never seen before. However, she had managed to harvest some fine specimens. So she gathered up her knife and the final pieces (she was delighted by a soft, rosy, threadlike

Bonnemaisonia, which was in very good condition), and laid them carefully in her bag. She tied the bag to her waist. She looked around for her hat, which had fallen off so often she'd discarded it, tethering it under a stone in case the wind caught it. It was soaked through, so she didn't put it on her head as she set off towards Duncan.

The rocks had formed a flat plateau, so she walked easily until she got to a wide gash in the surface. Earlier, she'd stepped over what had been a small stream, but now the water had come in, silently, smoothly. What was only a trickle now looked deep, perhaps over her knees. She didn't mind wading, but she could see the water was swirling: the currents were strong. She would prefer not to lose her footing. They were quite some way from their hotel and it would be a long walk if she was drenched. Perhaps if she went along the edge of the channel towards the cliff, she'd be able to find an easier place to cross. She set off, and when she got to the cliff, she found that the stream had carved a small inlet under the rock, over which a ledge jutted out. It wasn't too narrow; she could edge along it. She tucked up her skirts and prepared to clamber.

'Flora!' Duncan was on the other side of the channel, hopping anxiously. 'Are you all right?' Flora laughed, pushing her hair out of her eyes.

'I've been collecting! I've had such an afternoon. Wait till I tell you what I've found!'

Flora saw his smile vanish.

Duncan didn't look worried anymore. His eyes narrowed and a couple of patches of red appeared on his cheeks. He was gristly, she thought, like a cylindrical red rhodosperm.

'Don't step there. You'll fall. Wait.'

The commands were curt. He took off his jacket and laid it neatly on the rock. He unbuttoned his trousers.

'Duncan, I can do it! There's a shelf, look. I can manage, but it would be easier if you held out your hand, I can catch hold...'

He was in his long johns now and his undershirt. He glared.

'Stay there,' he snapped, and he stepped into the water.

It was up to his thighs. He struggled to find his footing. She could see that the rocks were slippery under his feet.

'You should have been keeping watch – tides come in fast here. You're a fool, a little fool,' he said as he waded towards her. Now it wasn't just his cheeks that were red, but his neck too.

'You're getting soaked. I can get along the cliff if I cling to it, you don't need to—' But he was scrambling onto her side of the rocks and, without asking, he picked her up and slung her over his shoulder, knocking her bag off her waist as he stepped straight back into the water.

'Duncan, wait! My bag!'

It was only about five big strides to cross the channel, but the water was coming in fast.

'What bag?'

'Duncan, do go back!'

'There's no time.'

'But it's full of my specimens!'

'Specimens!' He spat the word as he deposited her on the rocks on the other side of the channel. 'What are you talking about?'

'I-I-I've been collecting seaweed.' Her teeth were chattering. She was frightened of this cold man in front of her.

'I woke up. You weren't there. I was worried,' he said. He pushed her onto her back and pinned her arms to the rocks. 'And you. You were collecting *seaweed*.'

'I-I should have told you. It was a surprise. I have a collection. I put them in a scrapbook. I found some new ones today. I can identify them – there's a woman, an author and a scientist—'

'A woman scientist.'

The grasp on her wrists got tighter. He was lying on her with his full weight.

'She's an algologist. I wanted to show you what I'd found – I thought you'd like it – please, you're hurting me...'

She struggled to free herself.

'You thought I'd like a bag of old seaweed!'

'It's to add to my collection, my samples. So I can be an algologist too.'

The pressure on her wrists lightened.

Duncan rolled off her and onto his back.

She heard a sound. She wasn't sure what it was. She sat up and looked at him. He was laughing.

She struggled to her feet. She pushed her hair back, trying to capture the locks that had escaped her pins, and tucked her shirt back into her skirt.

'I want to be a scientist too.'

Duncan stood up. He let his gaze travel from the top of her head down to her feet.

'You. You want to be a scientist,' he said. 'My dear. You should take care. With that...' He pointed to her foot, the distorted, disfigured foot at the end of her shorter leg. 'With that you are very, very, *very* fortunate indeed to be a wife.'

He'd never mentioned her foot before. Of course she knew he'd noticed it; everyone noticed it as she walked along with her odd rolling gait. It made no difference to her everyday life, but she knew that men took it into account when they met her. It had meant she didn't have as many suitors as her sister, who was a lot less clever and whose eyes were really quite piggy. But her legs were both the same length, and her feet were sturdy and dependable.

'You should remember to be grateful,' Duncan said, 'that I took on damaged goods.'

He pulled on his trousers, then his jacket.

'Make sure I never see you in those disgusting boots ever again.'

He strode away across the rocks, back towards the beach.

*

She stood on the edge of the channel. She should follow him – of course she should. He was her husband.

But she could see her bag of seaweed lying on the other side, just out of reach.

It was not fair of him to have made her leave her specimens behind.

He might not immediately accept her ambitions, but maybe in time she could change his mind.

If she didn't obey and follow him back to the beach, she had no doubt she'd have to face his anger. She'd not yet seen Duncan angry, but she already knew him well enough to be wary.

If she gave in now, she'd have a lifetime of subservience to look forward to.

She looked up and down the channel.

There was one place where the two sides were closer together, perhaps close enough. The water was deep and churning here.

She stood on the edge.

You need to be brave and determined to be a seaweed hunter.

She looked at her husband's back as he stalked away from her. She looked at the bag of seaweed, sitting so tantalisingly close on the rocks.

She jumped.

ISLA

THE OUTSIDE-IN HOUSE

Skye, 2021

Isla is bending over the toilet bowl. She's scrubbing and scrubbing as hard as she can and she's poured as much bleach as she's got left in the bottle onto what should be pure-white porcelain, but it isn't. Not yet. There's only one thing for it. She takes a wet wipe in her yellow-Marigolded hands and reaches in.

Yuck.

She is actually scraping up someone else's shit.

Yuckyuckyuckyuckyuck...

She tosses the wipe into the bin and presses the chrome button. The water flushes round the bowl and swirls away, leaving the china sparkling. She's been told the loo has a state-of-the-art centrifugal flushing system that makes it particularly ecological and efficient. She doesn't care. It doesn't make it less full of crap. Isla swallows the bile that has risen in her throat. One more to go.

Isla always starts with the bathrooms. She can tell what kind of people have been staying straight away.

These particular visitors were careless and spoilt. The surfaces are covered with dollops of shampoo and moisturiser; toothpaste is spattered in the his-and-her basins. *They've been used to having people clear up after them*, Isla thinks, as she picks up the wet towels from the floor and takes them down to the washing machine. She'll have one wash on the go while she strips the beds.

She loves this house. It's a new build, an architect-designed love nest for two Danish guys who've made a fortune in logistics. The house is wood and slate and glass, and it looks over the sea. Isla pauses as she walks through the open-plan living area. It feels like the house is at one with the environment, like the outside is coming in. That's what Isla calls it: the Outside-In House. She leans against the plate-glass window and stares out. Rain is gusting over the moors, and the mist is heavy, grey and low. The sea is pewter with white tips on the waves. She can't see the flat-topped mountains on the other side of the bay. *When the mist is so thick you can't see Macleod's Tables then, like as not, it's set in for the day*, she thinks – and then she catches herself. She never used to notice the weather beyond deciding whether it was a sunscreen or a brolly day, and as for the landscape, well, there wasn't much landscape on view in the backstreets of Chippenham. She realises she likes it. She likes the light and the dark, the passing of the seasons, how each day is different, if you're paying attention. She even likes the mist, which is lucky, considering how much of it there is. She's begun to notice the shapes and colours of the hills, and has surprised herself by enjoying exploring them. She was beyond chuffed when she hiked up to the Quiraing, those strange twisting spikes of rock with their swards of emerald grass. She thinks they look like they've come straight out of *Lord of the Rings* – they're probably only populated by elves or fairies. Blimey, fairies! The island is getting under her skin.

Smiling to herself, she grabs the remote and clicks. She's still enough of a townie to enjoy modern gadgetry, and the Danes do like their gadgets. Salsa fills the air, and Isla swivels and shimmies as she climbs the stairs to the bedroom.

She was interviewed by the house owners on Zoom. They seemed nice. Friendly. Quite fastidious and careful, specifying what cleaning products they wanted used, pointing out how expensive this surface was or that sculpture. They've got a few carefully placed pieces that accentuate the perspective and the way the light enters each of the rooms. Well, that's what they said, anyway. On the whole, Isla has ignored their cleaning advice but admires their taste.

It's changeover day, and this is her third and final house. The others are old-style cottages, with faded floral cushions and mismatched crockery. She likes them – they feel lived-in and homely – but this one is her favourite, so she always finishes here if she can. There are no visitors booked in so she can take her time. She strips the big double bed – her second-least-favourite task. She takes care not to look at the sheets, whipping them off and throwing them into a pile at the door. As she pulls on the clean duvet cover, Isla focuses on the huge abstract that hangs over the bed's headboard. It is simple, just a streak of charcoal on a grainy background. There is something satisfying in the curve, a richness and a flamboyance. The shape starts as a thin line at the bottom of the canvas, then swirls up into a thick substantial body until it ends, flicking round and back with a final curl. *A rearing horse*, thinks Isla. *Or a wave. Probably a wave. How can something so plain be so beautiful?* She realises that she's buttoned the duvet cover all wonky, so she starts again. The pictures have not been hung for her.

Isla doesn't mind cleaning the kitchen. It is smooth and sleek and minimalist. She quite enjoys wiping the long, expansive surfaces, buffing the crystal wine glasses until they shine and placing the handcrafted fruit bowl in the exact centre of the granite worktop. She also likes the perks. She opens the fridge. A plate of half-eaten cheeses, some floppy, slimy salad and – bingo! Nestling in the door, an open and unfinished bottle of champagne. *Who doesn't finish champagne?* Isla decides to take a break.

She kicks off her shoes, lies back on the sofa and has a long swig. None of this is quite what she had imagined. She has been on Skye for four months now. She has a few cleaning jobs, including this one, which pay minimum wage. She has a couple of shifts at the petrol station shop, covering Chrissie's maternity leave. She's not earning much, but she's getting by, living cheaply. She could pick up some hospitality work if she wanted; there's loads around. She's loved exploring the island, and everyone she's met has been friendly, much more so than down south. She's got some mates – Moira, who works at the castle and is a proper laugh, and Dan, a climber and tour leader, who has rusty curls and a roguish smile. She's going to meet them at a party later. It's always fun on changeover day – everyone has stories of the visitors. She hasn't seen Luke again, the man who caught her swimming naked in the sea when she first arrived, but that's a good thing. She's glad she hasn't had to face him, although she would like to stop thinking about him. She takes another swig.

It's just that she feels she's not really living. She's passing the time. She's existing.

She stares around the room. There's another of those charcoal pictures. This one is a circle. Again, it is a shape which isn't quite complete but seems to be in perpetual motion. She gets up to examine it more closely. She runs her fingers over the curve, feels the fierce energy of the movement. She tries to imitate it, swooping her hand along the shape again and again as if it is hers, as though she is the creator. She heads for the sleek drawers in the corner of the room. She knows that there are craft materials in there, for the guests to enjoy on their holidays. She finds paper and, yes, there's charcoal. She sits at the kitchen table.

A curve. She can use muscle memory. It can't be that hard.

After five sheets of paper have been covered with meanderings, insipid and vague, Isla gives up. She scrunches up the papers and throws them at the overflowing bin. Turns out it *is* hard. She gets a bin bag out of the cupboard. She'd better get on with the cleaning. Looks like that's all she's good for.

But as she empties the rubbish into the bin bag, she slips the charcoal bar into her backpack.

*

Isla glides the Dyson over the pale-grey floor tiles. She's had this feeling before. This feeling of marking time. Of pressing her nose against a window and watching as everyone else lives their best lives. It's what drove her to come up to Skye in the first place, to leave Chippenham, friends, family, the safety of what she'd always known. Skye is definitely different. It's only her that has stayed the same.

She shouldn't wait for life to come and knock on her door. She needs to get out there. Take action. Any action.

As she fits the nozzle on the hoover to get into the corners (the Danes were very particular about the corners), Isla glances through the tall side window out onto the slate terrace. She pauses, Dyson whirring; she bites her lip and grins. She thinks about Dan and how his hand brushed hers last week, how the hairs on her arms shivered, how his eyes always linger on her, how he gives a crooked smile when he sees her. She's not encouraged him. Yet. *Hmm*, she thinks. *Maybe*. A plan begins to form.

When the house is spotlessly clean, she packs up her cleaning materials into a large red bucket to take home. But she doesn't put in the champagne as she had intended. Instead, she drops a teaspoon into the neck of the bottle to preserve the bubbles, and puts it back in the fridge door.

*

She's late getting to the party that evening – it takes her a while to get rid of the smell of bleach. There's always a gathering to go to here and she's always invited. There's no pub in the village anymore, so people make their own entertainment. A few weeks ago it was her turn, and her cottage was filled with locals and visitors, laughing at the stag, drinking beer and whisky, and dancing to her grandfather's old records. It had been fun. Tonight they're all at Euan-the-Potter's place: a white house on the edge of the village with a glass conservatory to keep them safe from the midges.

Euan is outside, leaning on the blue recycling bin and smoking, when she arrives.

'All right, Isla,' he says.

'How's the potting?' she asks. It's one of the things that has surprised her. Every second person here seems to be a potter or a weaver, a knitter or a painter, and every other house a studio or a workshop. That, and the fact everyone has at least three jobs. She notices that Rob the plumber is at the party. His ambulance is parked up. He doubles as the local paramedic. *A man for all your emergencies*, she thinks.

'Sold a couple of my big bowls today,' says Euan.

'Good on you – that'll keep you in whisky and cigs,' she says. 'Is Dan here yet?' Euan raises his eyebrows.

'In there.' He jerks his head. 'With a couple of Italians from the campsite. Got plans, have you?' He winks. Isla rolls her eyes and goes into the house. There's music blaring from some speakers, and knots of people are standing and chatting, or lounging on the sofas. Isla nods and grins at a few of them as she puts down her six-pack of lager and bottle of Talisker. She opens a beer and makes her way to Dan and Moira, who are in the corner with two blokes she's not seen before. They must be the Italians. Isla considers them. They are both good-looking, but Dan is cute too. He's got a tanned outdoorsy thing going that makes him look like a hiking advert. So what if Moira has told her he's a bit of a player? Isla's encountered Dans in her life before.

'Evening all.' She smiles. After a few introductions and basic info – the Italians are from Turin; yes, they're in a camper van; yes, they're on holiday; yes, they love Skye, so wild, so empty – she turns to Dan. 'So, Dan. What have you been up to?'

Dan has been out on the Cuillins all week, apparently, pitting himself against the peaks, leading a group of teens on their first big climb. He tells a complicated anecdote about rock crevices and crampons that Isla doesn't entirely follow. Instead, she lets herself wonder how hard he has to work to keep the six-pack she reckons lurks under his hoodie. When he's finished, Isla tells them about the Outside-In House and the champagne in the fridge.

'Come on! They'd hardly drunk any of it,' she says when Dan raises his eyebrows. 'I bet you get big tips when you manhandle your tourists down those crevices.' She smiles as she drains her bottle and goes to get another one. Dan follows her.

'Up for a sesh, eh, Isla!' he says. He grins and puts his arm over her shoulders and squeezes. 'Count me in!'

There's a moment when she could step away. Where she could turn lightly and run her hand through her hair, and so brush off his arm and let it fall, and she could smile and clip open a beer and hand it to him and no feelings would be hurt.

She knows it; he knows it.

So when she doesn't step away, when instead she leans into his chest, they both know that a line has been crossed.

*

An hour or so later, the party is winding down. Moira, Dan, Isla and the Italians stumble out into the night. The mist has blown away, and the sky is clear and full of stars. Isla throws her arms wide and stares, drinking it all in.

'They're so close,' she says. 'Like you could reach up and pick a whole bunch of them.'

'That bright one's the North Star,' says Dan. He stands very close behind her and takes her hand to point.

'Yup. And there's Ursa Minor, looks a bit like the Plough, then Cassiopeia – it's faint but it's there. And over to the left you can see Mars.'

'That's me told.' Dan laughs. Isla shrugs.

'Books and binoculars and nothing to do in the evenings. My grandfather must have had a thing about stars.' A few months ago she wouldn't have had a clue.

'You're full of surprises,' says Dan. He bends his head and kisses the base of her ear, featherlight. She lets him spin her round and kiss her deeply on the lips.

'Whoa,' says Moira when they come up for air. 'I reckon we should leave you guys to it.' She turns to the Italians. 'Got any whisky in your van?' They grin, and the three of them step off together into the night.

'I've got an idea,' says Isla.

'Me too,' says Dan.

'The Outside-In House!' says Isla, and when Dan's face falls, because that's not what he had in mind at all, she grabs his hand and pulls him along. 'Come on! I've got a surprise!' She leads the way to her car, which perhaps she shouldn't be driving, but it's not far and, anyway, she feels completely fine. She sees a van which looks familiar, with a man sitting outside it, a man she recognises, and when he raises his hand to his forehead and says, 'How do,' she realises it's Luke and her stomach lurches.

He's back, she thinks. *From wherever he's been. But I'm with Dan now. I'm with Dan.* So she smiles and nods, and she carries on to her car and gets in and Dan gets in, and they lurch up the road to the Outside-In House.

The house is black against the dark sky and Isla hesitates for a moment. This place is special to her. It's a sanctuary. Then she thinks of her plan to live life to the full, and she gets the keys out of her pocket.

'This way,' she says, leading Dan through the kitchen.

'Should we be here?' he asks.

'There's no one booked in. Don't be a wuss! The owners are in Denmark, you know they are,' says Isla. 'I think I deserve a bit extra after what I cleaned up today. I'll pop in tomorrow, tidy it up.' She leads Dan out through the side door. 'But now, it's time for a treat.'

There, in a curved enclosure open to the stars and with a view of the sea, is a hot tub.

'The visitors left it on. And I... didn't turn it off!' says Isla as she pulls away the cover. The water steams gently. She presses a button and bubbles erupt.

She looks at Dan, daring him. He doesn't need another prompt. He strips off and takes a running jump, hurdling into the tub.

Water cascades over the deck. Isla forces down the urge to mop it up.

'Hang on a mo,' she says and she nips back into the kitchen. She comes out with the champagne, some glasses and a couple of towels. She pulls off her clothes and clambers into the tub, sinking up to her chin in the water. Dan pours two glasses.

'Look at us,' says Isla. 'Bubbles, bubbles, everywhere!' She stares up at the stars. It's like they are dancing just for her.

'Come here,' says Dan, and his voice seems to have got quite a lot lower all of a sudden. Isla slides over and winds her arms around his neck. *This is how it should be*, she thinks as she kisses him.

*

It's probably because of the champagne, or maybe the bubbles, or perhaps it's something to do with the stars, but Isla and Dan don't hear the car. They are first aware that people have arrived when they hear a shout.

'Oi! What is happening?' It's a man with a faint Scandinavian accent and a mop of blond hair – a furious man.

'Get the *fuck* out of our hot tub!' he shouts, as another, darker man comes round the house behind him. They are both tall and elegant, and they both look very tired. They must have been travelling for hours. Dan and Isla scramble to get out of the tub and wrap themselves in towels and grab their clothes.

'How did you get in?' shouts the dark-haired man. 'Who are you?'

Dan drops the champagne bottle as he tumbles out of the hot tub. He squeals as he steps on the broken glass.

'Hey! What's your name?' shouts the blond man as Isla hops on one foot, looking for her shoes. 'Answer me.'

'Look, I'm ever so sorry. We weren't doing any harm,' says Isla, scooping up her jumper and scampering through the kitchen.

'You!' The dark man turns on Dan.

'I didn't know you were... It wasn't my idea, don't blame me,' says Dan, clutching at a towel. 'It was her!'

'Who is she?'

'Isla Wintergreen!' Dan trails blood as he runs through the kitchen. 'Your cleaner!'

'Ah yes, I know her face! The maid!' shouts the dark man.

Dan stumbles out of the door into Isla's car. Isla glares at him before she reverses sharply and drives fast down the drive.

'You dobbed me in it!' she says. 'We'd have got away with it!'

'They recognised you!'

'No, they didn't.'

'It was nothing to do with me!' says Dan.

'You were there! You jumped right into that tub.'

'It was your idea. You fucked up. Admit it,' says Dan.

'I just wanted to have some fun.'

'We were having fun. We didn't need to break into someone's house.'

'You were enjoying yourself.'

'They could call the police.'

'They won't call the police!'

'There's blood everywhere. I've got glass in my foot. And I might get a criminal record. Thanks a bunch.' Dan hits the dashboard hard. 'You can't just rock up here out of nowhere and expect us all to fuck up our lives cos you want to sit in a hot tub.'

'I thought you wanted to,' says Isla. 'I'm sorry.' Her voice is very small. She is swallowing tears.

'Look. Just drop me home,' says Dan. He turns his back on her and stares out of the side window.

Isla pulls up to the cottage that Dan shares with his mum and dad and two younger sisters.

'Here we are,' she says as Dan gathers up his clothes and opens the door. He steps out gingerly.

'Do you want a hand?' says Isla.

'No,' he says as he limps up the front path.

'Will I see you tomorrow?' says Isla, and the minute she says it she wants to claw it back.

Dan looks back at her. He doesn't say a word as he unlocks the door and goes inside.

All Isla had wanted was to feel something. To feel alive. And there was a moment in that hot tub, under the stars, with the bubbles all around her, when Dan pulled her towards him and she felt a wild tingling excitement that she hadn't felt for a very, very long time.

Then it all spectacularly backfired.

And Dan threw her to the wolves.

Isla cries herself to sleep.

*

When Isla wakes up, she feels a darkness lowering over her.

She's done what she always does. She's pushed things too far and then they've gone wrong. She closes her eyes. She'd be better off leaving. She hears her mother's voice: *Running away like you always do*. But she's messed everything up and everyone will hate her in the village for disturbing the delicate balance between the islanders and the incomers, the second-home owners. They'll be on Dan's side. She'll never get any more work and they won't speak to her when they see her. Just as she was beginning to be accepted, beginning to make friends, beginning to be part of a community.

She feels so ashamed.

She'll hand in her notice on the jobs and she'll leave tomorrow.

She stares at the ceiling. Maybe she'll have a swim. It might be her last chance.

She forces herself to get out of bed and open the curtains. It's a brighter day today. Outside, at least.

She pulls on her wellies over her PJs and grabs a towel. She goes down to the water, strips off her clothes and dives fluidly off the jetty.

She swims. Her strokes are strong and even. Her muscles have strengthened since she arrived; her swimming has improved. Maybe she could get a job here as some kind of swim guide, lead wild swimming tours of the bay.

No. She's leaving.

Dan will have told everyone what she did, and if he doesn't, the Danes will. They'll all hate her. It's not the way to behave.

Maybe she can stay until the end of the week? If she's selling the cottage, it seems a shame to go right away. She doesn't need to talk to anyone; she won't go into the village. She can work out her notice at the other houses. Clean them really, *really* well. Finish her shifts at the petrol station. She doesn't want to leave them all in the lurch. Like she usually does.

She gets out of the water and towels herself dry. She does feel better. Not great, but better. She walks up to the cottage and lets herself in. She puts the kettle on and steels herself to look at her phone. She wonders whether it was such a good idea to get Wi-Fi at the cottage after all.

There are lots of messages.

One from the Danes. *You are dismissed from your job with immediate effect for gross misconduct. We will be withholding your final pay cheque to cover the cost of draining and cleaning the broken glass around and in the hot tub.*

Fair enough. At least they hadn't called the police.

One from Moira. *What did you get up to last night??!! Are you OK?*

One from Euan. *Wow! Wild! Respect!!!* Really?

Another from Moira. *Hear you went to the Outside-In House. Hot tub spectacular! Call me!*

Another from the Danes. *Please return our keys with immediate effect.* What's all this 'immediate effect'? What's wrong with 'now'? And she doesn't have their keys – she chucked them on the kitchen counter as she left.

Finally, one from Dan. She takes a moment before she opens it. *Hey. Sorry about last night. Until they turned up I was having fun. Are you OK?*

Relief floods through her.

They don't all hate her.

Maybe she's not completely worthless.

Maybe she doesn't need to run away. Or not yet.

An hour later, after a hot shower and a hotter coffee, Isla sits down at the table. Perhaps there's another way to feel. One that doesn't involve champagne and housebreaking and a man who doesn't have her back.

Her backpack is on the chair. She unzips the pocket and takes out the charcoal. She's seen a pad of drawing paper somewhere. She scrabbles around and finds it.

She opens the pad on the first page. How would she draw last night's stars? How about the bubbles? She holds the charcoal flat and starts to sweep it across the paper. How about a fish? How about water? Her movements become smoother, more assured. The clattering in her mind begins to still, to focus, to calm. The shapes start to look, if not recognisable, then at least a bit more certain. A bit more like actual shapes.

Her phone pings. There's a message.

Hey Flipper. It's Luke. You're all about the scandal, aren't you? Quite the disruptor I hear. I have the use of a boat next week. Join me?

Luke. The man from the van.

She swirls the charcoal over the paper and creates a wave cresting before it crashes down onto a beach.

She smiles.

CATHY

SANDCASTLES
AND MERMAIDS

Weymouth Beach, 1998

'It's a scandal, that's what it is,' said Jim as he hauled the deckchairs down over the sands. 'Prioritising residents like that, over visitors. The deckchairs should be one price for all.'

'It's just a deckchair, Dad,' said Cathy, weighed down by a large cool box and three picnic rugs.

'It's the principle of the thing,' said Jim. 'I've a mind to write to the council.'

'You should do that, love,' said Pat as she plodded after her husband over the sand. She was carrying a parasol, a blue-and-orange windbreaker, and a large white beach bag spilling striped towels, buckets and spades. 'I'm getting too old for this, Cathy. Can we park ourselves?'

'I want to keep away from the Punch and Judy. Dunno how he's still allowed to be there, whacking away at his wife with his truncheon,' said Cathy.

'How about between that bloke with the tattoos and the yellow-umbrella family?'

'Right you are,' said Pat. 'Although, I do like a Punch and Judy myself, makes me smile. That dog chewing the sausages! It's not like it's real.'

'Free deckchairs! If that's what they call equality then I don't know what's what.'

'But we've got our own chairs, Dad, so it doesn't matter,' said Cathy. She took a deep breath, counted to three and exhaled. 'Shall we set up here?'

It was not until they put down their chairs, parasol, windbreaker, picnic rugs and cool box that they noticed that Isla was not there.

'Isla? Isla!' called Cathy.

'Where's that girl gone now?' said Jim. 'She was right behind us—'

'You stay here, Dad. Mum, can you try over there? I'll go that way,' said Cathy as she ran back the way they'd come.

'Honestly, that child will do my head in,' said Pat as she struggled up the sands towards the promenade. 'Isla! *Isla!*'

*

Cathy found Isla peering through a wire fence at a tableau of leaping and tumbling sea creatures frolicking around a half-naked man with long curls, all of which were carved out of sand.

'There you are, lovely,' said Cathy, hugging her too tightly in relief. 'I couldn't find you.'

'Look, Mum. It's a man with dolphins and mermaids and a stick.'

Cathy kissed the top of Isla's head.

'I think he's meant to be Neptune,' she said. 'He's the god of the sea. That's his trident.'

'Can he tell the waves what to do?'

'I expect he can.'

'Cool,' said Isla.

'It's clever, isn't it,' said Cathy as she looked at the sculptures. 'Amazing to build all that out of sand.'

'Who made it?'

'I don't know,' said Cathy. 'A sand artist. He's always been here. Shall we give him some money?' Isla nodded and they threw a few coins into the enclosure.

'There's his lunch,' said Isla, and she pointed at a sand apple and a half-eaten sand sandwich, perched on a ledge.

'And his dog,' said Cathy, nodding at the sleeping sand collie, curled up with his chin on his paws in the shade.

*

By the time they got back to their spot, Jim had hammered in the windbreaker – although there wasn't a breath of breeze – and Pat had laid down the rugs. She was sitting in one of the deckchairs, while Jim secured the umbrella.

'Where did you get to, young lady?' he said to Isla. 'I had to do all this on my own.'

'She wasn't far,' said Cathy. 'But next time, sweetheart, keep close. It's easy to get lost on a beach with all these people.'

Isla nodded.

'Now, who wants a swim?' said Cathy.

'Last one in the water's a jellyfish!' said Jim, pulling down his trousers to reveal some startling orange swimming trunks.

'That'll be me, then,' said Pat placidly. 'I'll stay here, keeping an eye.'

'Come on, Isla, race you!' said Jim. The tide was out, so he and Isla – who had on a poppy-splattered swimming costume, one of her favourite items of clothing ever – charged down the beach and ran on and on and on towards the sea, which was very far out. Even when they got to the water, it was only a few inches deep. It was warm and gentle, the waves nibbling at their ankles as they splashed in. When the water was up to Isla's knees, she lay down.

'I'm going to swim now,' she said.

'Right you are,' said Jim and he lay down in the water too, using his elbows to propel himself out.

Cathy, who had decided not to run half a mile across the sand in her swimming costume in order to dabble her toes in the water, saw the two heads, one blonde, one grey, bobbing above the shallows. She watched as Isla clambered onto Jim's back so that she could play at being Neptune, and Cathy let all the irritation with her dad's fussing and her mum's stolid dullness fade away.

*

After a lunch of pork pies, hard-boiled eggs, cucumber slices, tomatoes, crisps and very melted chocolate biscuits – Pat and Jim liked a traditional beach picnic – Pat went to sleep, and Jim and Isla set about building a sandcastle.

'We need to plan it first – we'll draw the shape,' commanded Jim as he scraped away the froth of dry white sand to get to the hard layer beneath. 'I'll mark the boundaries and you can start digging the walls there.' He pointed, and Isla obediently started to fashion the ramparts.

'What about the people?' she asked.

'We need to make the structure first,' said Jim. Building the structure took a long time, as it sprawled beyond the boundaries, and needed more walls and gates and ditches. Jim had bought Isla a special moulded bucket that made a tower with battlements if the sand was bashed in really well and it was turned out in exactly the right way, and he was using it to make sure that the castle was properly fortified. After a while, Isla drifted away and scraped at the frothy white sand to make her own hard patch. She started to mould a shape. It had long hair and a long tail and arms and legs, and it was recognisably a mermaid.

'Mum, can I have the eggshells?' said Isla, digging into the cool box.

Cathy was lying on her front, sunbathing, reading a magazine.

'Course,' said Cathy.

Isla crumbled the crushed eggshells onto the mermaid's head to make her hair. She put slices of cucumber on the tail as scales. She weighed down a plastic bag with sand to make shiny waves and she used a Coke can to mark out a frame of circles, as if the mermaid was in a picture.

'Isla? What are you doing over there? We've the moat to dig!' called Jim, still intent on the castle. 'Isla?'

'Coming!' said Isla, who wasn't and didn't.

'Time to float her!' said Jim, busy with the deep hole that he had dug in the middle of the keep. 'Fill up them buckets, Isla, love. Go straight there, straight back.'

So Isla skipped across the sand to the water, which was a bit closer now the tide was on the turn, and she filled the two buckets. As she came back, she picked up a couple of tiny pink shells like fingernails, a long thin shell her grandad called a razor, and a larger scalloped shell that she was particularly pleased with. She popped them all in the bucket and sloshed her way up the beach.

'You took your time!' said Jim. 'Pour it in, then!'

Isla tipped the bucket into the moat, but she must have tipped too hard, because a section of the wall crumbled and collapsed.

'Blimey, look what you're doing,' Jim said. 'It's taken me hours, this!'

'Sorry,' Isla said and from where Cathy was lying, she could see her head droop. Cathy stood up and shook herself down.

'Let's have a look,' she said and she surveyed the ramparts and towers of an extensive medieval village. 'Oooh, that's a castle and a half.'

'Just need a few of those flags you used to get,' said Jim. 'Then it'd look fit for a king.'

'Or a mermaid! Look at what I made, Mum!'

Cathy walked over to Isla's sculpted mermaid.

'I've found these, Mum, look,' said Isla, and she decorated the mermaid's hair and dress with the shells.

'Oh, that's beautiful,' said Cathy. 'And a cucumber tail! Useful if she gets peckish. She's a very lucky mermaid.'

'Why are you bothering with that, Isla, pet! Castles are what you build on beaches. You don't go around making a mess with a load of old plastic,' said Jim.

'Dad!'

'I want to be a sand artist when I grow up,' said Isla. 'Then I can make mermaids all day long.'

'Sand artist! What kind of a job's that?' said Jim. 'Lazy layabout, more like.'

'Dad, please! Isla, that's a lovely idea. Miss Gibbs is always saying how good you are at art.'

Jim snorted.

'Dad, leave it. She's only seven. Let her dream.'

'You've got to nip some things in the bud, Cath. Artist, my arse.'

Cathy could see tears welling up in Isla's eyes, so she clapped her hands. 'Right, rounders, now,' she said. 'Mum, wake up! We need you. Dad, you be bowler. Isla, grab the bat – we'll make a pitch over there. Come on!'

The family scrabbled for the rounders bat and ball, and for pebbles to mark the posts, and they paced out the pitch in the sand and Isla stood waiting to hit the ball and run as fast as she could to get a rounder, and Cathy thought, *Phew, another crisis averted*.

But as she walked past Isla's creation to the new rounders pitch, she wished she'd brought her camera. It really was a very beautiful mermaid.

*

When they'd played rounders and had another swim and had a go with the frisbee and bought ice-creams and dropped one of them in the sand, they started to pack up the camp to go home. They were collecting up their rubbish and Jim went over to the mermaid. He pulled up the plastic bag that Isla had used to make the waves. As he did so, he took a step back and his foot landed squarely on the mermaid's face.

Isla shrieked.

'Sorry, Isla love, I lost my balance—'

But he couldn't finish because Isla ran at him and pushed him, right in the stomach. Jim toppled over, falling hard on his hip.

'Oi, you little bugger, just you wait...'

Isla turned and ran off along the beach.

'Are you all right, Dad?' Cathy pulled him up.

'I'll survive. You go after that brat of yours.'

'She's not—'

'I could have hurt myself. A fall, at my age! Go on, or we'll be here all night.'

Cathy had already set off. She could still see the poppy costume dodging through the families who were left. The crowds had thinned out but there were still a lot of people on the beach.

Cathy wasn't worried. She knew where Isla was heading. As she jogged, she worked out what she'd say. *Grandad didn't mean it, he was only trying to pick up the plastic so we didn't leave rubbish on the beach; it was a lovely mermaid; pushing Grandad was wrong, though, he's getting on.* Or should she start with that? *Grandad is getting older, you shouldn't push people, you know that.*

Cathy got to the sand artist's display and looked around. She couldn't see Isla. She walked along the whole of the wire enclosure. Isla wasn't there. Had she climbed inside? It looked pretty secure, but maybe she had wriggled through the fence. Cathy peered in. The tableau of sea creatures that were so cheery earlier looked sinister and menacing, their faces frozen in grimaces and snarls. The long shadow from Neptune's trident seemed vicious and threatening. There was no little girl in a poppy-splattered costume.

She wasn't there. Where was she?

Cathy did a full turn, scanning the beach. She couldn't see her daughter anywhere.

'Isla! Isla!' Cathy started to run haphazardly through the crowds.

'Have you seen a little girl? She's got long blonde hair?' Cathy was panting now as she ran past family after family. One man tutted as Cathy tripped over his beach bag, knocking his towels into the sand.

'Watch it! You need to look after your kids. You don't know who's out there!'

Cathy ran on.

'I can't find my daughter! I can't find her!' she shouted at a woman about her own age.

'I haven't seen her,' said the woman as she hugged her own child close.

Cathy was crying now, tears streaming down her face as she shrieked for Isla.

'Please, please…' she panted.

'Here, love, I'll give you a hand – what's she wearing?' It was the bloke she'd seen earlier, the one with the tattoos.

'Thank you, thank you – she's about this high.' Cathy held up her hand to her chest. 'Pink-and-white swimming costume, blonde hair.'

'Right you are,' he said. 'Oi, Dave!' He called to a man in sunglasses who was on his phone. 'You go that way, I'll go down to the water. Make sure she's not heading out to sea!'

Cathy stared at him wide-eyed.

'Joking.' The bloke swallowed. 'She's probably gone to the swing boats, eh? The kids love 'em. Why don't you take a look? Dave and I'll search round here. What's her name?'

'She's called Isla,' she called back as she set off. The swing boats. Of course! The fairground area, with the trampolines and the helter-skelter – that's where she would have gone. Isla adored the swing boats! They hadn't been this time; she must have decided to take herself there. That's where she'd be!

'Isla, Isla, Isla!' Cathy shouted as she stumbled and tripped her way along the beach.

'Isla! Isla! Isla!' She could hear voices echoing around her and in the distance, as more and more people joined the search.

She was nearly at the swing boats. They were hanging in a long, multicoloured row. Only one of them, the green one at the far end, was rocking gently, backwards and forwards. There was no parent standing beside it. Someone inside had to be making it move – it must be Isla! Cathy ran towards it, sobbing with relief.

'Isla!' She grinned through her tears as she peered into the wooden boat.

Two teenagers were entwined at the bottom of the boat. The girl opened her eyes for a moment and glared at Cathy. She stuck her middle finger up at her before turning back to chew hungrily at her companion's mouth.

Cathy stepped away. Isla was not here. Not at the sand artist's enclosure. Not at the fairground. Cathy had no idea where her daughter was. Ice ran down her spine and shivers along her arms. Where had she gone? She could be anywhere. Which way should Cathy run? Where should she look?

'Are you the mother?' A police officer in a high-vis jacket was struggling across the sand towards her. 'We've had a report—'

'She's run away, she's run – I don't know where she is. She's only... she's running... I don't... please, please...'

Cathy couldn't speak.

'All right, all right, take a breath. We'll find her – kids run away all the time. She'll have gone to get herself an ice-cream or some sweets, like as not.'

The officer's voice was soothing but Cathy knew Isla hadn't gone for an ice-cream. She knew something bad had happened. Deep inside, her blood was curdling.

'Give me some details and then we'll sit down and have a cup of tea. I'm sure we'll find her in no time.'

She'll have run into the sea and she'll have drowned. It's not deep, but if she ran right out and into the waves...

'She's seven. She's got blonde hair. She's wearing a swimming costume with poppies on it.'

'Name?'

'Isla.'

She'll have run across the road and a lorry driver will have been looking at his mobile. He won't have noticed her because she's so small and he'll have tried to brake but it won't have been in time...

'Got a picture?' the officer asked.

'I haven't got my... I've... My bag...' Cathy couldn't get the words out in a proper sentence.

She'll have been taken. Snatched. He'll have seen she's on her own and he'll have grabbed the opportunity; he'll have scooped her up and put a

*hand over her mouth to stop her screaming. He'll
have bundled her into a van and slammed the door
and got into the driver's seat and...*

'All right, deep breath, and another, that's right.'
The officer pressed a button on her walkie-talkie.
'I'm Sheena, I'm going to stay here with you.'

From a long way away Cathy could hear Sheena
giving out Isla's details. A bit of Cathy thought how
crisp and efficient she was. Cathy wondered how
many people Sheena was talking to, how many
people would be looking.

Then Cathy went back to thinking of Isla swallowing seawater, of the water going into her lungs, of
Isla's body bloated and swollen.

Of Isla's body crushed by the full metal force of
an HGV.

Of Isla screaming in pain.

Of Isla being held in a dark basement—

'Mrs Wintergreen? Mrs Wintergreen.' The officer
was speaking slowly and clearly to her.

'Yes?'

'Will you come this way? One of my officers has
found a child matching Isla's description. She's alive
and well.'

Cathy seemed to be sitting down in the sand.
Sheena put out both hands and pulled her up.

'Is she, is she, is it... Isla?'

'We think so.'

'Where is she? Can we go...'

Sheena held Cathy's arm as they walked fast along the beach. Cathy didn't seem to be able to stand up and walk in a straight line by herself.

Beside the bandstand was a small group of policemen in those same high-vis jackets. They were grouped around...

'Isla!' Cathy found her strength and ran and ran, and grabbed Isla and swung her into the air, and hugged her and hugged her and sobbed and sobbed.

'I thought I'd lost you!' Cathy kissed her as Isla buried her head in Cathy's shoulder and looped her arms tightly around her mum's neck like she'd never let her go.

'She crawled under the bandstand,' said one of the policemen.

'Good hiding place,' said another, admiringly.

'She's a bit cold and shivery – she got scared,' said Sheena. 'Best to wrap her up and get her home now.'

'I will, I will, thank you, thank you,' said Cathy. 'Thank you so much.' And then she couldn't say any more as the tears were coming.

*

When at last they got home and all the recriminations and apologies were over, Cathy tucked Isla up in bed, hugged her hard and kissed her. Then she said:

'Please, Isla. Don't ever, ever run away again. I don't know if I could go through all that another time.'

'I won't, Mum,' said Isla, her eyes closing.

'Promise?'

'I promise...'

*

Even though she was very nearly asleep, Isla made sure to cross her fingers behind her back when she made her promise. *Just in case*, she thought. *It's not right to break promises, but it's OK if you cross your fingers first cos then it's not really a promise.* Isla didn't want to run away, not now; she'd been frightened on the beach. But she did think there might be a day – way, way in the future – when she might need to run away again.

MOUSSAKA

Chippenham, 2006

'I don't want it,' said Isla. 'I'm not hungry.'

'How can you not be hungry?' said Cathy. 'You've been at school all day!' She paused for a moment. 'You have been at school all day, haven't you?'

'*Yes*, of course I've been at school! Where d'you think I was? Do you want me to tell you exactly what lessons I had?'

'Go on, then.'

'Honestly! I can't believe you, Mum. Really? OK, we had Miss Watson for English first thing and she was soooo boring about – or, oh no, wait! I forgot assembly. I shouldn't miss out assembly, not if you need to get the full complete picture of my day. D'you know what Mr D said we should be thinking about this week?'

'What did you have after Miss Watson?'

'He said we should be thinking about *trust*.'

'How very appropriate. Miss Watson…?'

'*Mum!* Miss Watson double period, then break. Then Mr Grant double period maths. Then lunch, and I sat with Lex, but today lunch was gross so I didn't eat much, and it was sunny so we were outside. Then we had triple science. I had to sit next to Carrie.'

'How is she?' Cathy kept her voice flat.

'She didn't say anything. Wouldn't even look at me.'

Cathy reached out to touch Isla's hand. Isla snatched it away.

'Sounds like a tough day,' said Cathy.

'It was. I hate Wednesdays.'

'I know you do. That's why I made…'

Cathy gestured at the dish on the table. The moussaka was gleaming, the top burnished and shiny and fluffy-golden. She loved the way the eggs made the white-sauce topping rise, exactly like Delia said it would. Cathy's moussaka was pleasingly similar to the photo in *Delia Smith's Complete Cookery Course*, the book her mum had given her for her nineteenth birthday. Cathy had not been thrilled at the time. She'd wanted a Walkman.

'I didn't ask you to,' said Isla.

'Like I'd suddenly *not* make you supper one day?'

'I'm nearly sixteen. I can look after myself.'

'Well, that's true, and I always appreciate your help, but tonight I wanted to make you something special.'

'I don't want it,' said Isla again.

'It's your favourite…' Cathy knew this sounded whiny. But it wasn't as if she'd just put a pizza in the oven. The moussaka had taken time. And she'd also had a long day at work. She had hoped it would make Isla feel better about her fight with her newly ex-best friend Carrie.

'It might have been when I was nine! But I'm not nine now. It's full of carbs, all those potatoes, and look at the oil. I bet it's fried. Yuck! Anyway, I'm veggie now.'

'Right. Good to know.'

'I can't believe you eat meat, actually.'

'Like you did until today?'

'It makes me feel sick. You put something's *real flesh* in your mouth. It was alive and running around. It had *legs*. I mean. Just yuck.'

'Is Carrie veggie?'

'So what if she is?'

Cathy busied herself with the oven gloves.

'So what are you going to have now, then? If you don't want this.'

'I'll have a slice of toast. Or a bowl of cereal.'

'There're apples in the bowl. I think there's still a pear in there. Or you could have a couple of kiwis.' Cathy took out a serving spoon and settled down at the table.

'Can I have ice-cream?'

'No.'

'*Mum!*'

Isla cast her eyes to heaven, as if calling down all God's angels to support her in her trials and tribulations. Cathy dug the spoon into the crust and a heady combination of cinnamon, oregano, garlic and red wine filled the room, wafting her back to the seafront in Greece. She checked in with herself. Yes, the memory was now a poignant one, a pleasant pang of love long-lost, rather than the raw anguish she'd felt during Isla's early babyhood. She was relieved she was so well past all that now.

'Why don't you come down and get yourself something later?' said Cathy, as she ladled a portion onto her plate. Isla hesitated.

'Smells nice.'

Cathy put a forkful in her mouth.

'Mmmm,' she said. 'It is.'

'Maybe, like, a small portion?' said Isla.

Cathy dolloped one scoop onto the plate Isla held out. Then another, then a third.

'Can I take it up and watch telly?'

'Sure,' said Cathy, having won one battle. 'Bring your plate down when you've finished, and don't forget your homework.'

Isla skipped out and Cathy finished her moussaka alone. She put her plate, knife and fork in the dishwasher. Unlike her daughter, Cathy loved Wednesdays. Mum and Dad never missed the pub quiz at the Star, and she had the house to herself for once. Instead of cooking, she could have spent the time in better ways. Playing the clarinet.

Learning to dance flamenco. Painting a picture. She couldn't remember the last time she'd picked up a paintbrush... probably when she'd creosoted the fence last year. And she didn't own a clarinet. But dancing flamenco – perhaps that was doable.

She ran her finger along the CDs in the CD case and selected a Latin one she'd picked up in a charity shop a few months ago. There was a time when she and Isla would have put it on and danced around the kitchen together, giggling as they tripped over each other's feet. Isla wouldn't be seen dead dancing with her mum now. But Cathy could still dance, couldn't she? She put the CD in and pressed play. The music made her think of Mexico and tall, dark men with arrogant clicking fingers. She might not make it to Mexico, but maybe Mexico could come to Chippenham.

She started to shuffle around the room, wiggling her hips like they did on *Strictly*, as she pinged some clingfilm over the moussaka and slid it into the fridge.

ISLA

RUNAWAYS

Skye, 2021

Isla is sitting in the bow of a small wooden boat. She dangles her hand over the side, reaching her fingers down to the water. They are going fast, bouncing through the tips of the waves, and the spray splashes up at her.

'It's weird being on the water, not in it,' she shouts back at Luke. He is sitting in the stern, hand on the tiller, steering. He cups a hand around his ear. He can't hear over the motor.

This is the first time Isla's been out on a boat from the island. She thought she knew the coastline, but it looks different from the sea. Her section of coast looks flatter and less vivid, overshadowed by the drama of the moorland and the crags spiking up inland. There's so much sky. She can see her cottage. It looks insubstantial, huddling in the lee of the hill. It could do with a coat of paint. The bushes are crowding in on it – they should be cut back. Isla feels a pang. The cottage is part of the landscape, is part of Skye, and she is part of the cottage. *Home*, she thinks, and realises it's the first time she's called it that.

'Can we stop here?' she shouts.

'What?' Luke shouts back.

Isla holds up both hands. 'Stop!'

Luke cuts the engine.

'What's up?'

'Look where we are,' she says.

'Is that you there?' He points. She smiles. She knows he's thinking of her rising from the waves naked, after her morning swim. He catches her eye and grins.

'I thought we could try to catch a couple of fish for tea.' Luke opens a box by his feet and takes out two wooden handlines. He hands one to Isla.

'What do I do with this?' she asks.

'Drop the weight over the side, careful of the hooks, and unwind the line. I don't know if we'll get anything here but it's worth a try.'

Isla drops the line into the water. She thinks of the dates she used to go on back in Chippenham. Cider down the pub. Cinema on a Saturday night. A curry after work. She feels the wind in her face and tastes the salt on her tongue, and she looks at the man in the boat who is letting down the line into the water. There's something capable and economical about his movements. He looks comfortable in his skin.

They don't catch any fish. Luke shrugs.

'They must be somewhere else,' he says.

'I'm glad,' says Isla.

'We'll have to make do with sweetcorn,' says Luke.

'Where are we going?' says Isla.

'Wait and see,' he says, so Isla lies back in the prow and holds her face up to the sun shining faintly through the clouds, as Luke starts up the motor and steers the boat further along the coast.

*

After about a quarter of an hour they round the edge of an island and head into a bay. They chug towards a break in the jagged low rocks that jut out from the land. On the other side of the rocks, the water is glass-calm, lapping at a semicircle of silvery sand that sits at the base of tall black cliffs. Isla can't see any path down from the moorland to the beach; it looks like you can only get here from the sea. Luke inches the boat close to the shore and cuts the engine.

'Drop the anchor,' he says, and Isla throws it over the side. The boat bobs on its tether. Luke lowers himself into the water. It comes up to his thighs. He leans back into the boat and grabs a large yellow waterproof sack.

'Coming?' he says, and holds up his hand to steady Isla. She takes it, although she doesn't need any help. 'Careful, it's slippery.'

She finds her footing on the rocks. They hold on to each other as they wade to land. They are alone on the tiny beach.

'Magical,' says Isla, grinning at Luke. He smiles back.

'I do my best,' he says.

He takes a small camping stove and a griddle out of the sack. Some bottles of beer. A bag of food.

'I can't believe you brought all this,' says Isla.

'It was to grill the fish,' says Luke. 'I'm not sure that grilling sweetcorn cobs sends the same message.'

What message is that? wonders Isla.

'Me man. Catch fish. Feed woman,' she says.

'Me man, buy veg in shop, feed woman burnt peppers,' says Luke.

'I don't mind. Catching, killing and gutting a fish – then eating it – could be too real for me. Veg is fine,' says Isla. 'I might need a bit of time for the whole hunter-gatherer role-play.' And they smile at each other. It's easy, natural. She doesn't have to pretend.

Luke lights the stove and grills the sweetcorn. He's brought halloumi and peppers, some houmous and pitta bread.

'To the feast!' says Isla when they clank their beers together. She thinks that he's gone to a whole lot of trouble. It's thoughtful and kind, and she's pleased.

'My dad used to take me fishing when I was a kid,' Luke says, and he tells her how the family would come up to Skye from Liverpool in the summer and how different life here was from the city. How after his dad died and his mum hooked up with his stepdad, home wasn't much fun, and so he left as soon as he could. How he thinks of his van as his home now and how he picks up jobs as a gardener or barman or a labourer, whatever and wherever he can. How he never stays in one place for long. How he's alone, and happy with his own company, but sometimes... He looks at Isla. She nods. She knows what he means. Sometimes...

'What brings you here?' he says.

She tells him about the inheritance that came out of the blue, from her grandfather Hugh, whom she only met once and whose life is a mystery to her. How she doesn't know why he offered her a way out, but he seemed to have known, somehow, that she had always wanted to escape her home town, but never quite made it before.

'We're both runaways, then,' he says.

'But I'm running away to find my roots,' she says.

'How's that going?'

Isla looks out to sea. How *is* it going?

'I like it here. I like that I can start again, rethink who I am,' she says. 'And I really love the sea.'

He waits. She likes that about him. His stillness.

'There's a book in the cottage,' Isla says slowly. 'An album, really. It's old, from way back. It was made by my great-grandmother. She gathered seaweeds and washed them and laid them out in the album and labelled them. It's so careful and delicate. They're beautiful and mysterious. I've never looked at seaweeds like that. Six months ago I didn't even know I had a great-grandmother, and now I know I have one and she loved the sea too.'

He nods.

'It's like she's reaching down through the past to touch me,' says Isla.

He doesn't laugh. He doesn't brush her away or move on.

'I'd like to see that album,' he says.

*

It's a perfect afternoon. They eat and drink, they clamber over the rocks, they frighten each other as they explore the darkness of a cave, they build towers of flat pebbles, competing to see whose is tallest.

They are sitting on the sand when he asks about the faint blue ellipse tattooed on the inside of her wrist. Isla's skin shivers as though he has traced it with his fingers. She doesn't tell him the tattoo is there as a stop signal.

'What goes around comes around,' she says instead.

He doesn't kiss her.

The tide is on the turn. The shadows are getting longer. They pack up the food and the stove into the waterproof sack and sling it into the boat. Luke cups his hands in the water to give Isla a leg-up. She is nearly in his arms. But once she is in the boat, he lets go. She sits on the other side of the boat, to balance it, as he swings himself in. She pulls up the anchor, and he tilts the engine back into the water and starts it. They head out to sea.

She can't leave it like this. She doesn't want to leave it like this. One perfect afternoon. Only companionship from a man who seems to quiet the clamour in her head. Who makes her feel safe and secure. There must be more.

She is not sure why he hasn't made a move. Or why she hasn't. But there's not much time left.

The boat chugs up the coast until there is the cottage.

'Stop!' she shouts. This time he hears. He cuts the engine.

Isla stands up. The boat rocks. She takes off her life jacket.

'I'm going to swim home,' she says. Luke frowns.

'Are you sure? It's further than it looks,' he says.

'It always is,' she says, and jumps in.

The water is deep and cold and shocking. As she surfaces, she bobs for a moment. It does look a long way. Is this sensible?

But she's not sensible. She's wild and free, and she wants to feel alive.

Isla sets off at a steady front crawl towards the shore. She hears a vibration through the water, and she knows that it is the motor and that Luke is following her. But she doesn't want to give up; she doesn't want to be rescued.

She is used to the water now – it doesn't feel cold anymore.

She pauses and looks up through the waves. The shore and the cottage are closer. But they are still a way away. She looks back. There's the boat. She starts again. One, two, breathe. One, two, breathe. One, two...

She feels strong and sure. She is leading him, this man that she wants. It seems right. She is a selkie, gliding through the water. She is an ancient Greek nymph. She is a siren luring her man to the rocks, but in a good way. No wrecks here.

She is tiring now. She changes her stroke. Breaststroke means she can keep her head and her mouth in the air. The water is choppy – a wind is getting up. She can feel a dull ache in her hips. Her arms are getting heavy. She wants to rest.

She flips over onto her back and lies like a starfish. She stares up at the sky as she breathes. She mustn't float too long: the cold will seep in, her body temperature will drop, her blood will turn to ice.

What is she doing? What is she trying to prove?

All she knows is that it feels important. That if she can get to the shore, she will have achieved something and then Luke will be hers.

She swims on. It's harder now. Her body is a dead weight in the water. She is pushing herself with each stroke. Her head is not coming up above the surface as easily. A wave crashes into her face and she takes a mouthful of water. She coughs and chokes.

'All right? Want to get into the boat?' His voice is right behind her.

'Not far now!' she says and pushes on.

Is it not far now? She looks up. The shore is closer. It looks as close as maybe ten lengths of the swimming pool at home, not much more. She can do that. She can easily do ten lengths.

She's heard that when you drown, you just let the water come into your lungs. You breathe it in. You drown yourself.

One last push. She's nearly there. So nearly there.

One, two, breathe. One, two, breathe...

She can't lift her arms. She can't move her legs anymore. She can't even hold herself up. One leg floats down and... her foot touches some seaweed. She's not out of her depth! She stands and takes a breath.

She's made it.

She is swaying. Her legs are jelly. She wades towards the quay; it's only a few more metres. She's not sure she can take another step and then... she's there. She leans her arms on the jetty, lays down her head.

'Wow.' Luke idles the boat up to the concrete. He loops the painter around a metal bollard.

'That was some swim. I'm impressed,' he says. He jumps onto the shore and reaches down. 'D'you need a hand out?'

'I can manage,' she says and with her very last piece of strength she swings herself up onto the land.

'Here.' He throws a towel around her and gives her a hug. 'We need to get you warm.' And somehow the hug becomes closer, and he lowers his head and kisses her, and she knows it's going to be all right.

'Come up to the cottage?' she says. 'I need to warm up.'

She will never tell him how close she came to sinking.

She takes him by the hand and leads him up the lane to home.

HUGH

A BAG OF ORANGES

The Dead Sea, Palestinian Mandate, 1946

We're on leave. We have two days and the use of a jeep. We sling our kitbags in the back, throw in some beers and a big bag of oranges. We can't get enough of the oranges – we haven't seen them at home since before the war. Gil is whistling. It's the Django Reinhardt number that was playing in the club last night. Gil catches the rhythm. He's good.

We take a snap before we set off: my arm slung over his shoulder, the camp in the background, sand under our boots. We're in civvies. He's squinting; the sun's in his eyes.

Gil takes the wheel. I slide in on the passenger side, my shorts already sticking to the seat. The land is dry, the road all potholes and dust. There are camels and palm trees, a man leading a donkey piled high with bundles of reeds. It looks like the Bible. Unsurprising, I suppose – it is the Holy Land after all.

We stop in a village, a huddle of white houses. We drink freshly squeezed grapefruit juice and buy a bag of monkey nuts. The villagers laugh with Gil: his smile, that blond hair flopping over his forehead.

We're not supposed to stop. It's dangerous. We're targets.

We don't care. We light our cigarettes and lean against the jeep, and we think we're the kings of the world.

We're on our way to the lowest place on earth.

*

Gil Murray is a fellow officer in the Argylls, and my friend. He was posted to Camp 21 in the Palestinian Mandate a few months ago, joining us to 'keep the peace'. I was detailed to show him the ropes. I didn't find my duty unpleasant. He was confident and funny, a golden boy. I knew he would drift away once he found his feet. He would gravitate to the lads who laughed loudly in the club on a Friday night, lying about their exploits with the local girls. I would be back, marooned in the corner, with my beer and my books.

But he didn't drift away. He stayed. We played draughts together, and gin rummy, and held long chess tournaments using matches as prizes to while away our off-duty hours. And we talked. We talked and talked. Then:

'I'd like to go to Nazareth,' I said to him when I was due for leave. 'And Bethlehem.'

'I reckon they'd look like everywhere else,' he said. 'I want to go to the Dead Sea.'

*

It's a long way. The land scrolls before us: scrub and palm trees, orange groves, olive groves, settlements. We have a map and a compass, and we know we are nearly there when we see shimmering mountains in the distance and the glitter of water. A goats' track leads off the road, barely visible. The sea is turquoise blue and flat, and there are no waves. It's not what I am used to; it is nothing like the sea off Scotland.

We stop the jeep and scramble down the escarpment. The stones are sharp and slippery. I lose my footing and set off a small landslide. The pebbles tumble over each other down to the shore.

'All right?' Gil calls back to me. He is holding the bag of oranges and a canteen of water. I carry my towel.

There's no beach, only thick brown mud and stones. We strip off. I flex my toes in the mud, relishing the texture. My body is striped – blistered and red-brown on the arms and legs, white pale at my groin. My skin does not suit this climate. Gil is golden, his back toasted, his buttocks the palest honey.

We wade into the water. It is very clear. I scoop some water to my lips and retch at the levels of salt.

Gil rolls forward until he lies flat on the water's surface. He tries to make his legs drop down but they bob up. He laughs.

'Come on!' he calls.

I try to plunge in as if into a North Sea wave, but I can't. This sea is as buoyant as lying on a float. I flip onto my back and rest, looking up at the sky and the glare of the sun. I have never been in water like this. I imagine it's like lying on a cloud in heaven.

I glance over at Gil. He has laced his hands behind his head. I gaze at the lean length of his arm. The hairs at his armpit. The muscle that flexes on his torso. His slender foot.

I put my head under the surface to shake my thoughts away and it's a mistake: I shriek, the agony of salt in my eyes, the dagger-stings where I shaved this morning. I flail up; I thrash, gasping; I rub and rub at my eyes.

Gil is by my side. He is laughing again. He takes my arms. He pulls my face towards him. He puts out his tongue and gently licks each of my eyelids clean of salt. I blink. He looks into my weeping eyes. He leans forward.

He kisses me.

He kisses me on my mouth.

His lips are firm. They are hot. The inside of his mouth is burning and wet, and my body is on fire and it has nothing to do with the sun but everything to do with this man who is in my arms, his skin on my skin, his legs entwined in my legs, and it's wrong but it's right, so right, his lips on mine, his tongue in my mouth and on my neck and on my chest, my hands in his hair, on his body my hands.

After, we come out of the water, dazed and smiling and unwilling to let our bodies part. He throws himself onto my towel and bites into an orange, tearing at the peel, the juice running down his chin, and I am suddenly ravenous. I grab an orange and peel it with my teeth, and we find this so funny, we can't stop laughing until we silence our laughs with our mouths.

We pitch our tent near to the Dead Sea, in the shade of a couple of palm trees. No one will see us here. It is too desolate, too remote. We are private. We are alone.

*

The next morning, we crawl out of our tent and the sun is already high and hot in the sky. I am parched. I drain our canteen. I smile as Gil emerges, his hair tousled. I have no words for what I am feeling, for the bliss I felt last night, for the rush of warmth and – yes – love that I feel towards this man. I am awkward and gangly and pale, and he makes me feel like a god.

He runs a hand down my arm.

'We should head off,' he says.

I shouldn't ask. I need to know.

'When we get back…' I start, then hesitate.

'Mum's the word, eh,' he says. 'We'll have to lie low for a while.'

'Of course,' I say. 'It's dangerous.' I force something that might be a smile.

'Maybe we can try Jerusalem next time?' he says.

And the joy erupts in me because there will be a next time, he wants there to be a next time, and I nod, not trusting my voice.

*

We climb into the jeep and it's my turn to drive. We take the goats' path back to our road and we head west. We retrace our steps back through the olive groves and orange groves, and pass camels and donkeys and settlements. We sing all of the songs we can remember as we bump over the potholes. We sing 'Don't Fence Me In' and 'Run Rabbit Run', and we harmonise the choruses. We even sing the melancholy ones like 'We'll Meet Again', although we don't feel sad – we are ecstatically totally absolutely wonderfully happy.

We arrive in the village where we bought the grapefruit juice and I pull the jeep over to the side of the road. We are thirsty. Gil is swinging his legs over the door to the ground when there is a *crack crack crack* like a firework or a car backfiring, but that's not what it is because a small puff of sand appears in the road and I turn to look at Gil and he crumples back into the jeep as if he is a puppet and someone has cut his strings, and a red flower blooms on his forehead and it grows so quickly. Then there is another *crack crack crack* and the windscreen is a crackle of broken glass, and I pull Gil back into the passenger seat as I start the jeep and I am careering through the village, past the stall holders who had smiled so sweetly at us, and I am going much too fast but I need to get Gil back to camp, get him to a doctor, get him to hospital because maybe he has a chance, just maybe, if I am fast enough – and I have one hand on the steering wheel and one on him, and I need to get out of the village and away from the sniper, and I drive as fast as I can until the village is far, far away and just a dot in my rear-view mirror.

I stop the jeep. I get out and walk round to the passenger door. I open it. Gil slumps out, head dangling down, blood dripping.

He is dead.

I hold his body. I feel nothing. This is not Gil, not the man I kissed, the man I sang with, the man I loved. Moments ago this body was pulsing with life and laughter. Now it is empty. A shell.

I haul his corpse into the back of the jeep and lay him down, his head resting on the bag of oranges. By the time I get to camp, the oranges will be swimming red with his blood.

The powers that be kick up a bit of a stink when I get back. A British officer, shot in cold blood. Protests will be made, reparations demanded, arrests implemented.

I am numb. Useless.

I am not much of a soldier afterwards. They notice. I find myself demobbed, back on civvy street, and the world stays grey.

*

I keep the photograph. I put it in a frame. I look at him every now and again, squinting in that bright sun, his blond hair tumbling onto his forehead, and I see myself awkward and gawky, standing next to him, my arm slung over his shoulder. The pain remains dagger-sharp. I tuck the photograph away, somewhere hidden, somewhere safe.

I take it out again when I am an old, old man. It no longer gives me that original stabbing pain. I have covered that wound in layers over the years. I have lived another life, a different life. But I remember the Dead Sea and the skin on his shoulders smooth under my hands, his lips on mine, our legs entwined. I remember us singing as we bumped over those potholed roads. I remember his smile and I remember that he made me feel like a god.

Two perfect days.

Can that be enough for one life?

SINNING FOR THE
SAKE OF SINNING

A Watcher, Skye, 1973

I shouldn't be here, I know that. It's private land,
always has been, and just cos I want to see isn't a
good enough excuse, not in a court of law, not that it's
the most serious trespass, it's not like I'm a poacher
or anything, not that the man has deer or grouse or
anything other than a couple of sheep. I'm on the
rocks – my ma says they belong to everyone, it's below
the waterline that matters, she says. The tide's right
out anyhow and I'm at the far end of the headland,
standing over a load of old seaweed. Callum said he'd
spotted her yesterday and he laughed at me down the
pub – he said, wasn't I supposed to be the one that
knew all about birds and why hadn't I seen her, and I
said I'd go looking and he told me where. I borrowed
Da's binoculars, he'd never have allowed me, but he's
off on the boats right now, I'm only not there myself
cos of the mumps. So I'm scanning all the places where
she might have landed, I'm hoping for a nest – I know
a man who'd pay a ransom for the eggs, they're that

difficult to lay your hands on, and I've got the glasses up at my eyes already, so it's not like an intention or anything when I hear the car backfiring and revving as it comes down the track.

I swing round and it's a blue Ford Cortina and it's Mr Sutherland driving but I don't recognise the other man. He gets out and he's laughing and he's a sight, I can tell you, ever so fancy, he's got one of them bomber jackets and I can see it's leather, and cowboy boots with white jeans tucked in. The jeans are tight ones and they look like they've got jewels sewn on, there's all this glinting. Mr Sutherland's laughing too and I can hear their voices, they carry cos it's that still, and he's saying, *Adrian, you must come inside* and the other one, he says, *What kind of a love nest have you got here, you filthy thing?* They're right by the cottage where Old Tufty used to live till he died six months back, and Ma has been saying she doesn't know who'll have it now and it's a waste it just sitting there gathering dust. Then Mr Sutherland, he's looking in his pockets and he can't find the keys, and the other one puts his hand in the jacket pocket as if he wants to help and he's right up close to Mr Sutherland like he's going to hit him but that's not what he does. Mr Sutherland says, *Not here, not yet* and he looks round. I think he might see me or maybe catch the light off of the glasses, but he doesn't and he says there's a spare under the pot, and he's got the key and he's in the cottage and that other one, he's doing a proper skip in after him, then the door closes. The wee poofter.

My neck's hot and I'm sweating, I don't know why cos it's dreich out here. I'll not see one of them birds now so I make my way back and think I'll get on home while Mr Sutherland can't see me and get me in trouble, cos of how I'm not supposed to be on his land, but then I'm at the cottage and I crouch down and I'm under the window where Old Tufty used to have his parlour. I can hear them talking but not clear now, muffled, and then the voices are stopped so there's only noises and I put my head up where the curtain is, so as not to surprise them, and I look in.

There's no way what they're doing is legal, and Mr Sutherland a solicitor.

I don't know why I want to cry. My ma says my emotions are that up and down, I'm like a girl with her monthlies.

Then I think of Ma and how she stinks of fish all the time cos she never gets any time off from the gutting factory, and I think of how she looks old when I know she isn't and I think of how I'd like to buy her something to make her happy, maybe a colour telly, I know she'd love to have one, it would be that cheerful, or a bit of a holiday, Callum said the Costa Del Sol was proper when he went last year, he came back blistering red from the sun, he was proud as anything. Said he ate squid but I don't believe him.

Aye, I reckon I've found a way to buy that telly for my ma.

I reach into my bag and I take out my camera, state of the art it is, I bought it when I sold the owl eggs last year, I was that made up about it, and I put it up to my eye ever so slowly but I don't need to cos they are that busy and I take a snap then another then another, and then the other one, the one he called Adrian, he raises his head and he looks right at me. I click the shutter. I've still got that one, I look at it sometimes.

Then I run.

CONTENTS OF THE BLACK BOX
HUGH SUTHERLAND TOOK
INTO HIS CARE HOME

*Opened by Bram Sutherland after his
father's death, Inverness, 2020*

1. Items of uniform: two caps, worn. Bram later identifies these as part of the dress uniform of the Argyll and Sutherland Highlanders, from the 1940s. One has the name *Sutherland* written in the brim. The other has the name *Murray*.

2. A general service medal hanging on a ribbon with blue and green stripes. It has a clasp engraved *Palestine, 1945–48*.

3. Six thick bundles of letters, in chronological order and dated, tied with ribbons. Bram later identifies these as every letter, postcard and email (printed out and folded) that he has ever sent his father, beginning the year he started at prep school, aged eight.

4. Some loose photographs:

   A wedding photograph. Hugh and Mairi, Edinburgh, 1961. Mairi looks very happy.

   Sundry photographs of Bram, Mairi and Hugh on family holidays, sitting on beaches, having picnics, swimming.

A photograph of Hugh and Bram at the summit of Schiehallion, the summer that they decided to take hill walking seriously.

A photograph of a man wearing cowboy boots, white jeans and a bomber jacket. He has a kerchief tied around his neck. He has shoulder-length curly hair and is laughing. From the quality of the photograph and the clothes, it was probably taken in the 1970s. Bram does not recognise him.

A photograph of Bram in his prep-school uniform, holding a trophy. Bram remembers it was for cross-country running. He does not look happy.

A photograph of Isla, aged about seven, when she visited her grandfather in Scotland. She is wearing a flowery dress and sitting beside a stream. She is smiling.

5. Certificates. A practising certificate from the Law Society, Scotland, in the name of Hugh Sutherland. A marriage certificate between Mairi Lennox and Hugh Sutherland. A death certificate for Flora Sutherland, biological scientist.

6. A newspaper cutting: an obituary for a Michael Ferguson, dated 17 February 1986. Ferguson appears to have made a considerable sum of money from the illegal sale of wild birds' eggs, enough to build a new house near Portree, Skye.

He was arrested and charged under the Protection of Birds Act on a number of occasions and had a spell of imprisonment. He died of a suspected drug overdose. Bram does not recognise the name.

7. A red kerchief with white spots, ironed and folded.

8. A 1979 tide table for the Isle of Skye.

9. A letter from someone signing themselves *A Friend*. It is folded and creased. The words are nearly illegible. The sender has tried to disguise their writing and the ink has faded. The letter seems to be a demand for more money. It refers to intimate photographs. It is threatening.

10. A newspaper cutting: marked as from *The Times* (London, England), dated 23 July 1980. The cutting contains two articles. One has the headline *Crown Court Backlog Growing*. The other headline is *Commons Votes to Legalize Homosexuality in Scotland*. There is no indication which article is the most significant.

FLORA

CAMOUFLAGE

London, 1940

Flora Sutherland stood on the Embankment and contemplated the Thames. She'd always wanted to see it. It was thick and oily, the brown of milky tea, with currents swirling in its depths. Perhaps it wasn't at its best – barbed wire on its shores, concrete blocks to stop boats landing. She didn't think a concrete block would be that much of a deterrent if a boat had got up as far as Westminster, and she herself had cut through quite a few rolls of barbed wire since the war had started. She found wire cutters and a sturdy pair of trousers served her well if she wanted to get across a fortified beach to a shoreline. Flora turned round and stared up at the smooth white façade of the Shell building, now the Ministry of Supply, topped by the large black clock on its own plinth. Two fifteen. It was time. As she walked into the Ministry for her appointment with Major Braddock, she was looking forward to a lively and constructive discussion.

It turned out Major Braddock was not very concerned about the time. Flora was one of a number of ill-matched figures sitting on uncomfortable wooden chairs lined up in the pea-green corridor outside his office. The queue was moving very slowly. As she waited, Flora rehearsed what she was going to say. She was a well-known and well-respected figure in her university department, but this was different. She knew she must look old and shabby: her best black coat and hat had been smart enough when she left Edinburgh, but a much-delayed overnight train and tramping through London streets meant they were now creased and covered in smuts. She was also overloaded with baggage: her Gladstone bag and her canvas overnighter, as well as her wretched gas mask, which was a cumbersome beast at the best of times. She could see that she cut a strange figure from the sidelong glances her fellow queuers were giving her. She didn't believe any of this mattered. What mattered was what she had to say.

She had been sitting in the corridor for at least an hour and a half when the man in front of her exited the Major's office at a scurrying run, clutching a bunch of papers to his chest. The Major's secretary gave Flora a curt nod. She stood up and knocked on the Major's door.

'Enter!'

Flora went into the office. A man in uniform rose to his feet behind a large desk covered in neat piles of brown paper files, a shiny black telephone squatting importantly by his right hand. He looked weary, and Flora wondered if he'd been pulled out of cosy retirement somewhere in the Home Counties to do this job.

'Dr Sutherland?' Flora heard the surprise in his voice and saw his eyes sweep her up and down. She noticed that his gaze halted at her twisted foot in its ugly clumpy boot.

'Good afternoon, Major,' she said.

'I wasn't expecting—'

'A woman? People don't. May I sit?'

'Of course. Please.'

Flora took a seat. So did the Major. She rested her Gladstone bag on her knees.

'I'm here to talk to you about seaweed.'

She opened her bag and removed a package of greaseproof paper tied up with string. She unwrapped it, and rolled it out onto the Major's desk, revealing six strips of kelp. The Major grimaced, screwing up his nose. Even Flora had to admit that the smell of rank seawater was strong.

'It's been raining today, so the seaweed is wet. Seaweed predicts the weather most admirably.'

'Does it.'

'Seaweed is a marvellous substance. I want to talk to you about my research, about how seaweed can help you – help us, help the war effort—'

'You want to help the war effort with seaweed.' The Major raised his eyebrow very slightly, and sighed. 'This is a serious organisation, ma'am, looking for effective ways to combat our enemy.'

'I am aware of that, Major. You will be familiar with the work of E. C. Stanford, of course? His discovery of alginic acid in kelp, and the process of alkali extraction? We have been working on how to convert this into material—'

'Thank you for coming in, Mrs Sutherland, and for your… helpful… suggestion. This is not one for us.'

'But—'

'Good afternoon.' The Major stood up and held out his hand to Flora, to indicate the meeting was over. Flora wondered whether to argue, but he did not look like a man who would listen. She closed her bag.

'It really is remarkable,' she said. She walked out of the room and as she shut the door behind her, she heard him pick up the telephone to his secretary.

'What in God's name possessed you to let that bloody woman in here? Must we entertain every crank this country has to offer?'

*

Flora left the building and set off towards Embankment Underground station. The meeting had not been a success. She should have been downcast. She'd left Edinburgh with high hopes and a definite plan, and the Major hadn't even let her begin to tell him her idea. But she wasn't downcast – she was excited. She'd jumped at the chance to come down to London: she'd only been once before, and that was in peacetime. This was a different London, one she saw on the news when she went to the cinema, and heard about on the radio. Britain was a few months into the war and nothing much had happened yet, but this city was preparing for whatever the enemy might throw at it. There were silver barrage balloons in the sky; there were sandbags and kerbs painted white; there were ARP posts at junctions and soldiers in uniform jostling along the pavements. It really was most interesting.

Flora started to hurry. There was another reason she was excited. She had the address carefully written in her diary, but she needed to get there before blackout to have any hope of finding it.

She got out of the Tube at Russell Square and headed through the backstreets towards King's Cross until she found herself outside a down-at-heel lodging house sandwiched between a cobbler's and a tobacconist. This was where Thea Seymour lived. Flora had met Thea shore-hunting one afternoon at Portobello beach, over twenty years before. They had remained firm friends ever since, keeping up a regular correspondence by post. They met whenever they could, but years could go by without them seeing each other in person, particularly as Thea's work frequently took her away: she was an archaeologist at the University of London. She was ten years older than Flora, and she had become something of a mentor to her friend. It was Thea who had suggested a degree at Edinburgh University, and then a doctorate. It was Thea who had supported and gently chivvied Flora when she'd felt inadequate or overwhelmed. And it was Thea who had encouraged her to stand up to her husband Duncan. She had even suggested that Flora return to her studies after her son Hugh was born. Hugh had arrived when Flora had thought she was not able to have children and Duncan had long since turned his attentions elsewhere. Now Hugh was sixteen and away at boarding school most of the time. He had his own life. Flora believed she owed Thea a great deal.

'Flora, my dear! At last!' A woman with gunmetal-grey hair and a ready smile flung her door open wide. 'Come on up.' She ushered her up the stairs to the first floor. Flora looked around her. It was a bedsit, with a shared bathroom down the corridor. The windows needed painting and the walls were dingy, but the room was full of colour and warmth. There was a modern abstract hanging over the fireplace, orange and purple rugs lay on the floor, and some kind of bright red embroidered material had been thrown over the sofa.

'Syria, my last trip,' said Thea. 'Sit down!'

Everywhere there was evidence of travel and exploration. A chipped Roman vase held a bunch of hellebores. What looked like a small Greek goddess acted as a paperweight for some letters.

A few coals burnt in the fireplace.

'I'm saving them,' said Thea, following Flora's eyes. 'Coal will be on the ration soon enough, I imagine. We'll have to huddle up!' Flora smiled.

'I brought you a wee something,' Flora said and reached into her bag, pulling out a bottle of Talisker whisky.

'What a treat! Wherever did you manage to get that?' said Thea.

'Duncan's made sure his cellar's full. He's more worried about whisky than the Nazis. He thinks production will be limited soon, and then where will he be?'

Thea grimaced. She knew all about Duncan's fondness for whisky, and she knew what happened when he'd drunk too much.

'We'll have a tot after supper,' she said. 'You must be exhausted. All that way on the train, and then straight to the Ministry. We'll eat, and then you can tell me all about it.'

Thea busied herself at a small gas stove and soon put two plates onto the table. Cabbage, fish and boiled potatoes – straightforward enough, but Thea had brightened the fish with capers and lemon, and the cabbage with garlic and olive oil, bought in the bazaar in Damascus.

'The Middle East has spoiled my taste buds for the bland stuff that passes for food at home,' said Thea.

'What will you do now you can't go away?' Flora had long envied Thea's stints on digs in exotic locations. 'Aren't you going to miss it?'

'We're all making sacrifices and that's the least of 'em,' said Thea. 'Besides, I've got my hands full. I've never been so busy.'

'What are you doing?'

'It's all very hush-hush, but let's just say that they are finding a use for my languages!' said Thea. Flora had a stab of concern – might she be sent abroad? She must be too old for active service. Surely.

'Don't worry, I'm here for the duration,' said Thea and smiled. *It's like she can read my mind*, thought Flora. *I never have to explain myself.*

'Now. How did it go at the Ministry?'

'I brought him the sea in my Gladstone bag,' said Flora. 'But I don't think he liked it.' She told Thea about her meeting. Thea laughed.

'But in the end the joke's on me, because I didn't manage to tell him,' said Flora. 'So for all I think he was pompous and a fool, it was me who failed to get across how useful seaweed could be.'

'Hm. I've got a friend who works at that Ministry, down in the basement,' said Thea. 'Maybe you could visit him tomorrow. Explain what you're doing.'

'Do you think he'd listen?'

'More so than the Major. Although, keep that wretched seaweed off his desk!'

Thea poured them both a whisky.

'Now, tell me about my godson,' she said. Flora softened and smiled as she told Thea about Hugh, his love of history and of books, how handsome he was growing, how she was beginning to see the man in the boy. Then they talked of Duncan, and of Thea's parents, now elderly but hopefully safe down in Devon. They talked about the war and what might happen, and they talked of Syria and Persia and the latest discoveries in the desert, about seaweed and Flora's research and the ideas that she was pursuing with the team in her lab. Flora thought that she hadn't talked so much for months, even years – not since she last saw Thea, in fact. She wished Thea lived closer; being able to talk like this made her realise how lonely she was.

The fire had burnt itself out and a clock in the distance struck two in the morning when Thea stretched and yawned and said she had better turn in – she had to be at her desk by nine.

Flora felt a lump in her throat. She didn't want this to stop.

'You have the life I would have liked to live,' she blurted out. Thea was still for a moment. Then she leant over and put her hand over Flora's.

'You can live it too, if you choose to,' she said quietly. 'There's room here for both of us.'

There was silence for a moment, a charged silence where possibilities swirled like smoke. Then Flora drew her hand away.

'I'm a fifty-year-old woman,' she said.

'So?' said Thea lightly. 'Think about it.' She opened a cupboard and pulled out a pillow and a blanket, passing them to Flora. 'You're on the sofa, I'm afraid. Make yourself as comfy as you can!'

*

That night Flora lay awake. She turned over scenarios in her mind. She pictured herself living in London. Saw herself striding through the streets as though they were home. She'd never have to see Duncan's leering red face again, or feel his wet lips slobbering on her neck. She'd never have to suffer the indignity of knowing she was serving tea to his mistress. She'd never have to smile at his friends and listen to them talking about their deals, their wives and their golf. She could transfer to a university department down here. She could work any hours she chose. She'd have freedom to eat and drink and sleep whenever she felt like it, to entertain whoever she liked, to talk until two in the morning, or go to bed at teatime. She could fill her kitchen with kelp if she wanted to. And she would be with Thea.

When Flora eventually fell asleep, she had a fitful dream where she was running down a steam-filled platform, trying to catch a train that was just chugging out of a station. When she woke, excitement and dread churned in her stomach simultaneously, making her queasy.

Thea had left for work. A note was pinned under the small Greek goddess on the table.

I've telephoned Cecil. He's expecting you. Do consider my offer. Love, Thea x

Flora repacked her bag in a daze, clattered down the stairs and out of the building, and retraced her steps to the Ministry.

*

The meeting with Cecil Whitworth was very different to the one with the Major. Cecil came up to the foyer to meet her. He couldn't be that much older than Hugh, Flora thought. He was wearing rumpled Oxford bags and brogues, and his hair was as dishevelled as a dishmop: Flora itched to take a brush to it. He ushered her into his basement office and swept a pile of papers from an armchair so she could sit down.

'Thea says you know all about seaweed,' he said. 'Tell me.'

So Flora told him. How a sodium alginate fibre could be made out of seaweed, how strong it was and how versatile. Cecil looked at the kelp in her Gladstone bag and at the carefully wrapped package of alginate fabric that she pulled out. Flora explained how it could be used as a substitute for materials like cellophane, silk, or even jute. Cecil paced up and down as he told her how he'd read about research into alginates when he was at Cambridge. He asked her question after question about the extraction of the viscous algin material from the algae, how the mineral acid was applied and whether the process was completely stable. Then he told her about the problems the government was facing sourcing jute, as the sea passage from India became ever more hazardous.

'They'll be coming at us from the air,' he said. 'Everything needs camouflage. Airfields, hangars, factories. Everything. And camouflage is made from jute.'

Flora suggested that seaweed, readily available on any beach around the British Isles, could be the answer. She held her breath. Cecil agreed that the idea was worth further investigation.

When she came out of his office, Flora felt like punching the air. She'd done it! Her beloved seaweed was on track to help the war effort! And how much easier it would be for her to do this work in London – she'd be so much closer to the heart of things! How exciting it would be to be so meaningfully involved. She nearly skipped as she made her way to the Tube. She'd go back to Russell Street and wait for Thea to come home, and she'd tell her the good news. All the good news.

Flora sat on the Tube as it rattled through the darkness. She thought about Cecil. About his thin bony face, his mobile hands gesturing, waving his cigarette in the air, his enthusiasm and his boyishness. He reminded her of Hugh. As Flora changed from the Bakerloo to the Piccadilly line, her steps grew heavier. She thought of her son, his delicate face, his gentle smile. She thought of how fragile he was, how vulnerable, how easily bullied. She thought of how little sympathy there was between father and son, of how often she stood as a bulwark between them. She thought of Hugh, and when the train pulled to a stop at Russell Square station, she didn't get out.

When she arrived at King's Cross, she walked up out of the Underground into the mainline station. She saw on the departures board that a train for Edinburgh was due to leave in an hour. But before she could take it, there was something she needed to do.

She went into a café, sat down and ordered a cup of tea. She took out a pad of writing paper. She made many attempts to compose the letter. She wanted to excuse, to justify what she feared would be seen as a lack of courage, a failure to grasp an opportunity to escape. But it was hard to explain, to make someone understand how far she had come already, and how there were ties she could not, would not, cut. That there were people who needed her, even if they didn't know it, even if they didn't seem to care. How sometimes the brave thing to do was to stay.

The tea was quite cold by the time she wrote her final draft. In the end, she kept it short.

My dear Thea. Thank you for your kind offer. I cannot accept. With my love, Flora.

She folded the letter into an envelope, wrote the address on the outside and added a stamp from her purse. She gathered her baggage, the gas mask banging against her leg, and went out onto the station concourse where there was a pillar box. She posted the letter, then made her way to the platform where her train was waiting.

She stepped into the carriage and back to her future.

Tomorrow she would take a bus to Portobello and she would look at the sea and she would revel in its magnificence. Tomorrow she would go into her department and share the results of her meeting. Tomorrow she would start to do important and significant war work.

But today, just for a moment, she leant her forehead on the glass of the train window, and she let herself cry.

ISLA

COMING UP FOR AIR

Skye, 2022

Isla glides through the water, face down, her mask magnifying the world below. It's calm and clear today. The tips of the underwater gardens sway with the waves, and beneath them she catches glimpses of deeper weeds, shining and jewel-bright. She is fully neoprened up in her new wetsuit, and as she kicks her flippers, she feels gloriously like a seal, particularly when she dives down into the growth. But she's not hunting fish. She has spotted a perfect sample of seaweed. It is cherry-red and its branches are symmetrical and graceful. It is exactly what she has been looking for. She snips it off at the base and slides it carefully into her bag. When she resurfaces, she punches the air in triumph, even though there is no one to see. She heads for the shore.

*

Back at the cottage, Isla strips off her wetsuit and showers. As she dries herself, she wonders whether this is what her great-grandmother would have done when she was collecting for her seaweed album. Perhaps she rushed home and laid out her samples immediately, wrapping her weeds in towels to dry and preserve them. Was she hardier than Isla? She wouldn't have had a wetsuit and flippers. Isla wonders where she collected her seaweeds. In the album, she labelled her samples with Latin names; she took such care, wrote out the words in such a beautiful copperplate hand. But there were no dates, and no locations. It was as though her great-grandmother wanted to preserve the seaweeds, but not remember where and when she found them. Isla thinks about this sometimes. Wonders what it was she'd wanted to forget.

*

When Isla is warm and dry, she takes her sample bag into the kitchen. The counter is now set out with a line of mixing and baking bowls, repurposed for seaweed washing. She fills them with fresh water. She's competent and sure of herself. She's done this before.

She opens the bag and she takes out her seaweeds, careful not to tear their pin-thin tendrils. She admires her cherry-red treasure. She doesn't name it – she's not interested in lists and categories. She's interested in beauty.

She takes the seaweed and lays it in the water, gently swirling her fingers to swish away clinging sand or shells. One tiny mollusc drops to the bottom. She scoops the weed out and places it in the next bowl, in clean water. The weed floats, delicate, intricate, feathery. It's like a miniature oak tree in winter, all of its many branches and twigs exposed, empty of leaves. A fully grown cherry-red oak tree the size of her palm.

Isla slides a sheet of paper into the water and lets the weed settle. Using the paper, she lifts it out of the bowl, tilting it to drain the water away. She lays the sample on the counter. Now she should use a porcupine quill, if she were really following in her great-grandmother's footsteps. That's what Mrs Alfred Gatty recommends, and who would argue with the Victorian seaweed hunter extraordinaire? Certainly not Isla, but porcupine quills are not readily available in 2022, even from Amazon, so she uses a toothpick to spread the fronds of the weed and tease off any final dirt. As the weed dries, it will stick to the paper. She stands back to admire her work. It's exquisite.

She lays a sheet of muslin over the paper. Unlike quills, muslin was easy to buy, which surprised her until Maureen in the shop explained how to make bramble jelly. Isla takes the sample into the cottage living room, where the floor is now covered with piles of books and sheets of newspaper. She takes the front page of last week's *Herald*, lays it on the floor, places the sample on top. She piles on a tower of books. If she changes the muslin regularly, her sample should be dry in a few days.

As she stands up, she catches sight of the old album, open as it often is, this time on a display of *Rhodophyllis membranacea*, an intricate multi-branched specimen. Isla knows this page. She knows all of the pages. She's spent a lot of time poring over them. The seaweed is faded now into a sepia memory of seas long gone. But the shape is still there. A slender memory thread of cherry-red vibrancy.

Isla glances at the clock. She's going to be late. She pulls on her coat and grabs her bucket, full of cleaning products. She runs out to the car and sets off for work.

CATHY

SUNDAY LUNCH

Chippenham, 2022

Cathy arranges the purple crocuses in a tiny glass vase and puts them in the middle of the table. She's used one of Mum's favourite yellow tablecloths and chosen Mum's best china, even though some of it is a bit chipped and cracked these days. Sunlight floods the room, and it all looks warm and welcoming and springlike. She can smell the lamb roasting and catch hints of the rosemary and garlic she's rubbed into the joint. She smiles. It looks perfect.

The doorbell rings. *Trust Dad to be so punctual*, she thinks, as she takes off her apron and checks her hair in the mirror. She's looking forward to seeing him. She opens the front door.

On the doorstep is her father, Jim, dapper in a smart blue anorak with a dark wool cap pulled over his white hair. He looks well. He flings his arms wide.

'Cathy, love,' he says. 'Here I am at last!' Cathy grins.

'Hello, Dad!' He goes to hug her.

'Best not, eh,' she says. 'They come into the surgery with all sorts. I've tested, of course, but you never know.'

'Elbows, then,' says Jim and they touch elbows, smiling.

Up the path towards them walks a plump woman in a green quilted jacket and comfortable squashy shoes. She has grey cropped hair, gold-rimmed spectacles and a wide smile.

'I found a space round the corner,' she says. 'Hope it'll be all right there.' She holds out her hand to Cathy. 'I'm Barbara,' she says.

'Cathy.' Cathy offers her elbow again, puzzled.

'Let me introduce you,' says Jim. 'Barbara, this is Cathy, my daughter. Cathy, this is Barbara, my wife!' Jim puts his arm around Barbara's shoulders and she leans into him, as they both hoot with laughter. Jim gives Barbara a smacking kiss on her forehead.

Cathy's smile freezes.

'Wife?' she says.

'We got married two weeks ago!' says Jim. 'Happiest day of my life.'

Cathy resists the urge to slam the door in his face.

'You'd better come in,' she says, 'and tell me all about it.'

*

Cathy ushers the pair into the kitchen. The sun has gone in, and what had looked so glowing and fresh a few minutes ago now looks dingy and old-fashioned.

'Oh, crocuses, how pretty!' says Barbara.

'Barbara's got ever such green fingers,' says Jim. 'You should see her garden. It's a picture!'

'Is it?' says Cathy. 'I don't have much time for gardening, I'm afraid.'

'Jim says you work in a surgery,' says Barbara. 'You must have been run off your feet. However do you cope?'

Cathy feels a deep weariness. How has she coped? How does she ever cope?

'Do sit down,' she says. 'Can I get you something to drink?'

'Sparkling water, please,' says Barbara.

'Dad? Beer? Glass of wine?'

'A sparkling water for me too, love,' he says.

'Really?' says Cathy. Dad has never drunk sparkling water in his life.

'You'll need to lay another place,' says Jim as he pulls out a chair.

'So I will,' says Cathy. She tugs at a drawer so hard that all the cutlery rattles and bounces.

'Can I freshen up?' says Barbara.

'Up the stairs, on the left,' says Cathy.

As Barbara leaves, Cathy turns to Dad.

'What the bloody hell, Dad? How long's this been going on? Married? Why on earth didn't you tell me?'

'Calm down, Cathy, love!'

'Don't tell me to calm down! And – the best day of your life? What about Mum?' says Cathy.

'This has nothing to do with your mum.'

'Of course it does! How can it not?'

'For goodness' sake, Cathy, it's been two years.'

'Yes! Only two years! After how many decades of marriage?'

'Are you angry I didn't tell you or angry I didn't invite you?'

'Both,' hisses Cathy. 'And more.'

'But you like surprises,' says Jim, as Barbara comes down the stairs.

'I like a surprise bunch of flowers – not a surprise wife!'

'What a charming house,' Barbara says in the silence.

'Thank you,' says Cathy.

'Jim tells me this used to be the family home?'

'That's right.'

They'd all lived here: Mum and Dad, Cathy and Isla. There wasn't enough room, really, but they'd managed and it meant that Mum was able to help when Isla was a baby, and Cathy was on hand through Mum's long illness. After Mum died, Dad spent more and more time in his caravan down in Bournemouth.

Cathy had thought it was a phase. That he'd get bored of the sea and want to come home. But then, against her advice, he sold the caravan, and used every penny of his savings and more to upgrade to a one-bed retirement bungalow. And now he's done this.

She wonders if he's suffering from diminished responsibility. Whether this is the beginning of Alzheimer's. Whether she could get him certified. She wonders if she could get one of the GPs from the practice to pop round. Or one of the nurses. Someone. Anyone. Now.

'So. Tell me the story, then. How did you two... lovebirds... meet?' Could they tell that her teeth were gritted?

'Well, it's a funny story, Cathy, it really is,' says Barbara. 'We met on the internet!'

'An old codger like me!' Jim grins.

'Well, there's a surprise,' says Cathy.

'Oh, not like that! Not a dating site or anything. Your dad was organising a litter pick. He's got such a good community heart.'

'Aw,' says Jim, with what Cathy thinks is a disgustingly cheesy grin. If he doesn't stop pawing Barbara, she thinks she might be sick.

'A litter pick. How unusual.'

'Well, the beach gets so full of rubbish, and if you left it to the council, the whole place would be buried under a sea of plastic in a week!'

'That would be a tragedy.'

'And then he asked me out for dinner and, well, I couldn't resist.'

'Excuse me a moment, I've got to...' Cathy gestures vaguely to the oven.

That's the problem with open-plan – there's nowhere to hide. Barbara is warbling on about the dinner they had and Jim is chipping in with what the waiter said, and Cathy crouches down and opens the oven and wonders how soon it might be cool enough to put her whole head in.

'How's Isla?' asks Jim, when Barbara pauses in her commentary on the tenderness of the steaks and the very unusual flavouring of the tiramisu. Cathy feels her customary wave of sadness. Suddenly, she wants to see her daughter very much.

'She's still in Skye,' she says. 'At the cottage. Looks like she might stay for a while. I told you.'

'No, you didn't,' says Jim.

'On the phone, the other day.'

He's definitely got Alzheimer's, she thinks. She'll get a diagnosis, get this ridiculous marriage dissolved, get him away from Bournemouth and back here. She just has to work out how to do it.

'Oh yes, now you mention it. The place her other grandfather left her. Well, she'll have to wait a while to get anything from this granddad!'

Jim cackles. Barbara cackles. Cathy sighs.

'It'll just be a few minutes,' she says and she closes the oven. 'So, how did it all happen?'

'Oh, it was so romantic! We were strolling along the beach—'

'Was this before or after you'd removed the litter?'

Barbara laughs, obligingly. Cathy loathes her.

'After! There was nothing to get in the way of a beautiful sunset. And then – well, d'you want to tell her, Jim?'

Jim obliges, telling his daughter how he'd gone down on one knee, which was a bit of a mistake – he'd got his trousers wet because they were too close to the waterline – and he'd got out his ring...

Cathy tunes him out. No one has ever asked her to marry them. What is wrong with her? Doesn't she deserve love? She's had boyfriends, of course she has, some nice, some less so, but none of them were long relationships. She's spent years – decades – looking after other people, and now those other people are buggering off to Skye or getting their trousers wet when they go down on one knee to propose to someone in such an impractical place that, honestly, they're lucky not to have fallen over and drowned in the gently lapping waves of Bournemouth beach. That would have shown them – it's what they deserve.

Cathy realises Dad has stopped talking. Both he and Barbara are staring at her. She realises she's standing with the oven gloves on and that her face seems to be held in a kind of fixed rictus scream, perhaps a bit like Medusa. She rearranges her features into something resembling a smile.

'Go on,' she says.

'So, like I said,' says Barbara, 'I managed to get a dress at a very reasonable price in Marks, ever so smart...'

Cathy's away again. She hadn't had much choice, of course. Single mother, no help from Isla's dad, or that's what it had felt like. She'd had to come home, and once she was home, there was no way she could escape again. Perhaps she should have fought harder. Should have upped sticks and fled to London like Dick Whittington, only with a baby tucked under her arm. But staying seemed the sensible, responsible thing to do, and she had Isla to think about. It's not like she hasn't had friends and work colleagues and excitement over the years. Some excitement.

'Are you all right, dear?' she hears Barbara say.

'Yes. Of course. Fascinating,' Cathy says.

Dad clears his throat.

'So, like Barbara says, we need to make the arrangements.' They are both looking at her.

'What arrangements?'

'For the equity release. In this house.'

'What?' says Cathy. 'I've missed something here. You want to borrow money on this house?'

'Well, it is my house,' says Dad. 'And I might not have long left.'

'You look perfectly healthy to me,' says Cathy. Jim gazes at Barbara.

'We want to make the most of it.'

'And do what?' says Cathy. She can feel her cheeks burning.

'Well, we'd like a nice honeymoon. We quite fancy a cruise.'

'A cruise? Are you completely and totally out of your mind?' says – shouts – Cathy. 'You're in your late seventies, Dad. Those cruises are literally Petri dishes of disease! It'd kill you!'

'There are some good bargains to be had at the moment,' says Barbara.

'Oh, I wonder why?' says Cathy. 'You want to sell the roof over my head to go swanning round the world in some decadent dance of death!'

She sees Dad glance at Barbara and shake his head with a barely perceptible wink. So they're winking at each other now. They have secret messages. Dad has a new person to wink at. Cathy gets a lump in her throat.

'I think we'll talk about it another time,' says Dad. 'When we've got to know each other a bit better. No need to rush things.'

'Right you are,' says Cathy. 'Let me know when you want me to move out.'

'It's not going to come to that, Cathy, love,' says Dad. 'We don't want to put you to any trouble at all. You won't know the difference!'

Of course she would. Of course she'd know the difference. She'd only own half the house, the half that Mum had left directly to her. And when Dad died, and surely he'd not have that long left, she'd have to sell the house. Five minutes ago her sensible and responsible past meant that her future at least was secure. Now...

'Can we eat, love? We've had a long drive, we're starving,' Dad says.

'Yes. Of course,' Cathy says. 'I'll put the veg on the table.' She takes the roast potatoes, crispy and soft, cooked just the way that Dad likes, and puts them in a dish. She adds the parsnips and the glazed carrots. She drains the broccoli and tips the gravy into a jug. She carries it all to the table. She lays a place for Barbara, taking care to put the knife and the fork gently on either side of the mat, rather than slamming them down as she wants to do. Then she takes the leg of lamb out of the oven and puts it on the carving dish. It is a splendid joint, glistening and cooked to perfection. For a moment, she remembers what it feels like to be pleased, and how happy she was earlier when she put the meat in the oven. It was too big for the two – now three – of them, but she'd really wanted to give Dad a treat. Was that only half an hour ago?

'Here we go, Dad. It's lamb. Your favourite. A proper Sunday lunch.' Cathy forces a smile as she puts the roast on the table. She doesn't get the response she's expecting. Dad looks embarrassed; Barbara is squirming.

'I'm sorry,' Barbara says. 'Jim should have said. I'm veggie, have been for years. And I think I've managed to get Jim to join me.'

She smiles at Jim. He looks longingly at the lamb but says, 'Yes. Just the veg for me, thanks, love.'

Cathy looks at the table groaning with food that she's cooked. She looks at the couple waiting expectantly to be fed. She thinks of what they've said about meeting and getting married and going on a cruise and making the most of things, and rage starts to flame under her skin. It starts at her neck and surges all over her body until it consumes her, and she grabs the leg of lamb by the bone and with a deep guttural roar of fury she flings it at the window.

The glass shatters, and the leg of lamb flies out and lands in the middle of the small patch of lawn.

Dad and Barbara stare at her, frozen. Barbara holds on to her plate, in case it is going to follow the lamb. She looks shaken. Dad looks like he might be about to laugh.

Cathy feels fantastic.

Barbara leans over to Dad and whispers, but loudly because Dad is getting a bit deaf, 'Menopause,' and Cathy sees Dad nod.

But it is not the menopause. It is the years and years and years of caring and cooking and cleaning and wiping and worrying and planning, and it is the decision she has just taken: that she's going to stop. She's going to get a lawyer and she's going to make sure that Dad can't sell her home over her head. In fact, she might get some equity release herself and go on a cruise – or probably not a cruise, because she definitely thinks they are Petri dishes of disease, but on some kind of luxury holiday where she can lie in the sun and swim in the sea and relax and enjoy herself. Perhaps Greece. She hasn't been to Greece for many, many years.

She turns to Dad and to the woman who, she supposes, is now her stepmum.

'Get out of my house,' she says. 'Right now.'

FAMILY

A PICTURE OF A WHALE

Skye, 2022

Bram is driving over the bridge from the Kyle of Lochalsh to Skye.

'When you were a wee boy there was no bridge.'

'I know, Mum. It's been here a while now, though.'

'We'd go on the ferry to Armadale.'

'Yes.'

'You were always sick. You never could bear the motion.'

'No.'

'And I'd tell you to fix your eyes on the horizon to settle your stomach. But it never worked.'

'No.'

'I'd feed you a cracker when we docked and you'd be as right as rain by the time we got to the cottage.'

'Yes.'

Bram isn't seasick anymore. He hasn't been for years. But now he listens to these stories of his childhood afresh. He wants to pass them on to Isla. He wants to tell her about packing up their old blue Ford Cortina with suitcases and fishing rods and tins of corned beef, and driving across the mountains, crawling along the narrow roads, then piling onto the ferry and off again, and that hollow feeling of anticipation that was nearly unbearable until they arrived at the cottage, and he could tumble out and run down to the water and find every single thing that had changed. He wants this story to trickle down and be part of the warp and weft of her life. He wants her to know. He isn't sure why.

*

Isla stands in the middle of the room and surveys the pictures hanging on the walls. They look terrible. It all looks terrible. The flow she was so pleased with last night has gone. What was she thinking? The first piece people will see is a large abstract with layered stripes of light- and dark-green seaweed, and what had looked like an entrancing underwater portrait of movement and currents now looks like something you might find in a food waste bin. It's a terrible picture. She should take it down, chuck it in a skip. She should chuck them all in a skip. Why would anyone want to look at them, let alone buy them? Not that anyone will come – not a single person will come through the door.

'All right?' The voice behind her makes her jump. Luke is always creeping up on her. Startling her.

'No! I've got to redo it. We're going to have to start again.'

'We're opening in half an hour.'

'I don't care!'

He strokes her arm.

'Tell me what you need me to do,' he says.

*

Cathy has broken down. She is on the side of the road, beside some big lake or other, and the mountains are towering over her, and this was not what she had planned when she bought the camper van. Nic at work had told her that the old VWs were unreliable but she'd liked the look of them and thought that they'd be easier for her to drive than some enormous Winnebago. It's annoying that the van has broken down, but it's particularly annoying that Nic appears to be right. Why on earth didn't she buy a sensible Golf and check in at a Travelodge on the way up instead?

The AA man promised he'd be here in half an hour. He'd better be. At this rate she's going to be late. She kicks the tyre – the very flat tyre. As she does so, a cold wet nose nuzzles into her hand and she looks down at the daft ball of fluff by her side.

She picks up the puppy and gives her a kiss. She feels better. Nic was right about that too.

*

Isla's palms are sweating and her mouth is dry. Even the backs of her knees are tingling. She is standing by the door. She looks over at Luke. He is behind a table covered with a red-and-orange striped tablecloth and rows of cups and saucers, with gleaming glasses for wine or elderflower cordial. The refreshments cost her more than she'd expected, and she's not sure the cakes she made yesterday are up to any kind of catering standards, but she figures that even if the punters don't come for the pictures, they'll come for the tea. If anyone comes, that is. Luke gives her a big thumbs up and grins. She grins a wobbly grin back, takes a deep breath and opens the door.

Just outside, standing waiting, is her father. By his side is an elderly lady with a grey bob and a walking stick.

'Hello, Isla,' says Bram. He looks nervous. They haven't met since his disastrous visit to the cottage last year. But tentatively, carefully, they'd started to text each other, then to speak on the phone. Isla shared her anxieties about the exhibition – her first exhibition – and Bram was encouraging and reassuring. When she sent him the email inviting him to the opening, he got back to her straight away, saying he was delighted.

'Hi,' says Isla. 'Thanks for coming.'

'I'd like to introduce you to your grandmother,' says Bram. The elderly lady by his side smiles broadly and steps in to give Isla a hug.

'I'm Mairi,' she says. 'Let me look at you. What a grand girl – aren't you just gorgeous! This is an absolute pleasure.'

'Hello,' says Isla. 'It's – well, it's really great to meet you. Do you want to come in?'

She hooks the door open and stands back so they can step inside. The room is bright and light. Sunlight bounces off the rough whitewashed walls, bringing out the vivid colours of the pictures. They have been hung in groups of three or four, and there are about thirty in total, all created out of seaweed.

'Oh!' says Mairi. 'You're not telling me you did all of these yourself?'

'Yes,' says Isla.

'Well, they're beautiful!' She peers at the first picture, an exquisite cherry-red bloom. 'It's like looking down into a rock pool.'

'That's one of my favourites,' says Isla. 'I wanted it to be the first thing you see.'

'I can understand why,' says Mairi. 'Now, why don't we have a cup of tea and you can tell me all about yourself before your guests arrive? And then I'll have a proper look at your work.' She links her arm with Isla's and walks with her over to the tea table.

*

'There's no need to take that tone with me,' says the AA man. 'It's not my fault you hit a pothole and your spare is flat, too. It's illegal, you know. I could report you.'

Cathy thinks she might boil over. She controls herself.

'I know, I know. I'm sorry. I just need to be somewhere. I should be there right now. This has all taken so much longer than I expected.'

'It's all about the preparation. People set off on journeys without a thought, as if they've not a care in the world. No one bothers with the checks and then they land up in trouble. Happens all the time.'

Cathy looks around. There's not a village or a petrol station or even a house in sight, just open moor and this one-track road, snaking across to the sea. It looks a bit like the moon. Except with sheep. And wind turbines.

She has to be nice to this man. He's her only hope of getting away from here. She smiles.

'Is there anything you can do? Please.'

'Well, of course. I carry a spare in the van. Like I say, happens all the time. I'll get it on for you in a jiffy. You'll have to drive slow, mind, until you can buy another.'

Cathy loves the AA man. More than life itself.

*

Isla can't believe how many people have come. There's Moira, of course, arm in arm with her Italian, back for his third visit of the year. There's Dan, who has forgiven Isla for the hot tub and found consolation in the arms of an energetic rock-climbing Kiwi. There's Euan the potter, and Rob the plumber-cum-paramedic, who has parked his ambulance outside. There's Chrissie from the petrol station, her baby asleep in a sling; Maureen from the village store; the London boys who've bought the big house and are doing it up; and a whole host of other people, some of whom Isla knows by sight, and some she's never clapped eyes on before. She put an announcement about the opening in the local newsletter and it seems to have worked. The room is full of laughter and chatter, and a few people are even looking at the pictures.

'Excuse me, are you the artist?' A man in a thick green jumper and walking boots is standing in front of her.

'Um, yes. I suppose so.' He looks puzzled. 'Yes, I'm the... artist,' says Isla more firmly. She feels a swell of pride.

'I'd like to buy that one,' the man says, and he points at a small picture where the seaweeds suggest wild, swirling waves.

'It's £150,' says Isla. She squirms. She'd agonised over the pricing.

The man takes a roll of greasy £20 notes from his back pocket and leafs through them. He holds out a wodge of money. Isla looks at him and gives him a huge grin.

'You're my first sale. Ever,' she says.

'I like it.' He shuffles his feet. 'Makes me think of... well, it's got a smell of the sea,' he says. 'I'll bring the wife over later in the week. She can choose another.'

*

Isla is putting a sixth red 'sold' dot on a picture when Bram comes over. He's been chatting with the guests, many of whom remember him as little Bram Sutherland from years back. He's managed to make some introductions to Isla. He hopes it's helped.

'Selling well,' he says.

'I couldn't believe that anyone would want to part with actual cash,' says Isla.

'Have faith in yourself. The visitors'll love them too.'

'Maybe,' she says.

'I'd better get my bid in before you sell out,' says Bram. 'I'd like to buy that one.' He points at the collage of light and dark green strips.

'Really?' says Isla. He knows it's the most expensive piece at £600.

'I love it. I'll hang it over my fireplace at home.' As he says this, he realises that Isla has never been to his home.

'In London?'

'You'll have to come,' says Bram. 'Visit your picture.' He's careful. He doesn't want to push too hard.

'I'd like that,' she says.

Bram can't stop himself smiling.

*

There's a commotion at the door – a dog is yapping. Isla turns to see that Cathy has got here at last. She looks dishevelled and exhausted. She has a small dog with her, and the dog is having a poo on the doormat.

'Mum!' Isla runs over. 'You're here!'

'Hello, sweetheart. Sorry to be so late. Do you have a J-cloth or something? She's gorgeous, but I think she's got anxiety bladder...' Cathy is scooping the poo into a bag, but a pool of pee remains.

'You wouldn't believe the journey I've had!' she goes on. 'It's such a distance, isn't it? The motorways were OK, but coming up through Scotland took the time. I broke down – the AA came, lovely man in the end. I've got to get a new tyre, but that can wait!'

Luke appears with some wipes. Cathy cleans up the puddle. She gathers the dog up into her arms.

'This is Ginger, by the way. She's a Cavapoo – well, I think she's a bit of a mixture to be honest – six months and she's pretty much house-trained, although she did just forget herself, sorry about that, she's been an angel in the van. I parked it over there, do you think that's all right or should I move it?'

'Mum, this is Luke. He's my...' Isla looks over at Luke, who smiles at her. 'He's my boyfriend.'

'Oh, right, lovely – I've heard all about you,' says Cathy. She holds out her hand, then thinks better of it, as they all think about the dog. 'Good to meet you. Is there somewhere I can clean up?'

*

As Cathy crosses the room, she sees a man. The man looks very much like Bram would if Bram was twenty years older than when she last saw him. But what would Bram be doing here? He's staring at her. She frowns and walks straight past him. She doesn't look at the paintings. She walks into the ladies, goes into a cubicle and sits down on the loo, clutching the dog to her. Her heart is racing and she's sweating. She squeezes her lips together to try to stop herself crying.

'Mum?' The door clangs open. 'Mum? Are you all right?'

Cathy forces her voice to stay steady.

'Of course. Just having a wee. Out in a minute.'

'OK.' Cathy hears the door close as Isla leaves. She takes a shuddering breath. Then another. She can't stay in the cubicle forever, although that's what she'd like to do. She's going to have to face him. *You can do this*, she says to herself, *you can*. She wipes her face with some loo paper, pulls the chain and goes out.

Isla is leaning against the basins, arms folded.

'What's up?'

Cathy is still shaky. 'You didn't tell me your dad would be here. It was a bit of a shock, that's all.'

'I asked him. I didn't know if he'd come.'

'I'd have liked to prepare. I mean, look at me! I haven't even brushed my hair!'

'You look great,' Isla lies. 'Why not put on a bit of lippy, and come out?' She gives her mum a hug. 'Do you want me to help?' Cathy shakes her head. Isla leaves.

Cathy looks at herself in the mirror. She hasn't seen Bram for years. She'd have liked to be wearing something other than her driving trousers and trainers. She hadn't changed into the dress she'd brought, because she was so late. She wishes she'd washed her hair, had a shower, worn a bit of make-up.

Cathy sighs. She'll have to do her best with what's in her handbag.

*

Cathy comes out of the ladies and walks straight into Bram. He must have been waiting for her. She stands stock-still.

'Nice dog,' says Bram.

'She's called Ginger,' says Cathy.

'I heard,' says Bram. 'Can I?' He scratches her head, making a clucking noise.

The silence pools around them.

'How are you?' says Cathy at the same time as he says, 'How have you been?'

'You,' says Cathy.

'I've been better,' says Bram. 'But I'm loving all of this.' He gestures to the room. 'She's got talent.'

'I must look at them,' says Cathy, beginning to step away, but Bram touches her elbow.

'Will you come and say hello to my mother? She's always wanted to meet you.'

And Cathy can't say no, so she is propelled across the room to sit down next to Mairi and to be given a glass of wine, and to talk about her journey and her home town and the last few years and Isla's childhood, and if she wants to say: 'Your son abandoned me,' she doesn't; she can't find the space or the heart to do so.

*

Isla locks the door to the gallery. She is elated. She has sold more than half the pictures, on her very first day. So many people came, far more than she expected. All the wine has been drunk and most of the cake eaten. A man from the local radio has asked her to come into the station for an interview. A woman from an arts group in Portree has asked her to give a demonstration of her seaweed technique. And now she's going to go out to supper with her mum, her dad, her granny and her boyfriend for the very first time in her life.

She crosses the road to the restaurant. The others are already at the table. She slides in next to Cathy.

'All right, Mum?' she says. Cathy smiles. It's not a proper smile, but it is a smile.

'Well done, sweetheart. What a success! Not that I know anything about art, but I saw a lot of red "sold" dots on the pictures and that's got to be good.'

Isla leans against her. For the first time she realises how much she's missed her mother.

'A toast! Let's have a toast!' says Bram, and he sloshes wine into all of their glasses. 'To Isla! To her seaweed, to her art, to her life on Skye!'

Isla sees Cathy hesitate, just for a moment, before raising her glass. Isla leans over and whispers, 'It'll not be forever. Just for now. Just for a while,' and Cathy kisses her cheek.

'To Isla!' she says and she drinks.

'Thank you,' says Isla. 'Thank you all for coming. I love that you're all here. Before we eat, I've got one more picture which I want to show you. It's for a very important person.'

She takes a parcel from her bag. It's wrapped up in brown paper, with a ribbon tied around it.

'Mum, it's for you,' says Isla. Cathy takes the present.

'Unwrap it, then!' says Isla. 'Go on.'

Cathy pulls at the ribbon, and folds back the paper.

'Oh, Isla,' she breathes.

The picture is of two whales. The bigger one – the mother – has a smooth curved back formed out of one wide piece of seaweed. She is curling protectively around a smaller whale whose flippers and tail are going every which way. The bigger whale radiates calmness and steadiness, resting a flipper on the head of the small whale. The small whale is full of frenetic energy and vigour.

'It's us,' says Isla. 'It's you, looking after me.'

Cathy swallows. 'It's lovely,' she whispers. 'It's really lovely.' She turns the picture outwards to the table. 'Look, everyone. Isla's drawn me as a whale!'

*

The meal is long. The food is good, the wine is flowing, and the conversation is light and civil. When the last coffee has been drunk and the last mint chocolate eaten, the guests disperse.

Bram kisses Cathy carefully on the cheek.

'I wondered if you'd like to join my mother and me for lunch tomorrow?' he says. He's staring fixedly at his feet. Cathy checks in with herself to see how this feels. Unexpected. But not painful. It could even be… fun.

'Why not?' she says. Bram gives such a wide grin that he looks like a small boy. 'Tomorrow, then,' she says.

She makes her way unsteadily back to her camper van.

Isla is sitting on the steps.

'Come for a walk with me?'

'What, now?'

'Please…'

Cathy looks at Isla. Her hair falling in curls around her face, her crinkly smile. Her daughter. The surge of fierce love surprises her.

'Where do you want to go?' she says.

'Down to the beach,' says Isla. She points at a footpath that leads through a gap in the stone wall. It's a clear night and the fresh moon is bright enough to light their way.

'Where's Luke?' asks Cathy.

'He's around,' Isla says. Cathy follows her as they scramble down to the shore. The sea is black, and the sound of the waves lapping on the rocks is rhythmic and soothing. Cathy sees that Luke is already on the beach, and that he has built a fire. The flames are catching hold, and they light his face as he sits cross-legged on the sand.

'I wanted you to see it like I do. Like we do,' says Isla. 'To see how special it is here.'

Cathy looks. There is water and sky and stars. It is big and empty and quiet. There is space to live, space to be. She can smell the salt and see the moonlight reflected on the waves. She can feel how this might seep into your bones, how it might tug at you, like a current, pulling, insistent.

'I'm so happy for you, really,' Cathy says. 'You've found your place, you've found your passion. But...'

'I know, I know,' says Isla. 'You're sad too. That's OK.'

Isla turns on her phone and taps the screen. The music is pure and simple: a lament perhaps, a woman's voice using a language Cathy does not recognise, but who seems to be singing every conflicting emotion that Cathy is feeling. Isla holds out her arms.

'Dance with me, Mum? Like we used to do?'

Cathy laughs, although she's crying too as she steps into her Isla's arms. They dance a slow, gentle dance along the beach. As they move, Cathy thinks that maybe now is the time for her to find her own future, exactly as Isla has done.

The music fades and the waves come in over their feet, but they do not stop. They dance and dance and dance in the shallows, under the tender light of a newly born moon.

Book club and writers' circle notes for the
Fairlight Moderns can be found at
www.fairlightmoderns.com

Share your thoughts about the book
with #DancingInTheShallows

Also in the Fairlight Moderns series

ANTHONY FERNER

Small Wars in Madrid

David Aguilera's life is collapsing around him. After the catastrophic loss of the vessel under his command and a perilous trek across the Baltics to safety, he returns home to find himself unable to reconnect with his family. Frustrated by his inability to express what he is feeling, his wife Margalit moves out to stay with friends, taking their children with her. As David anxiously awaits the official inquiry into his conduct, he turns to those who are most important to him - his closest friend and colleague Marce; his Catholic adoptive mother; his Jewish birth mother; and Margalit, herself Sephardi Jewish.

Faced with the prospect of losing his family altogether, he must confront his conflicting identities and faiths and decide the man he wants to become.

'Small Wars in Madrid *is a thoughtful novel about trauma, coming-to-self, and the sometimes inextricable links between such complex processes*'

—Ilana Masad, author of *All My Mother's Lovers*